Michael's Bell

Jerome Flauto

ISBN:978-0-0578-11174-2

This book is dedicated to my wife Carole who has been my protector for over forty seven years. She is a constant reminder to me, that to love someone is a gift to be cherished, and that love can only be given from an unselfish heart. She and our three sons, Jerry Jr., Mark and Phillip have always encouraged me to tell the stories, and share the gifts that we receive. It is with great honor that I am allowed to share this story with all those who believe in the power of love, and harmony between man and nature.

Jerry Flauto

Cover Photographs by David Korow
Cover Design by Sri Rahm

Foreword

For over forty years "the call of the sea" has drawn me to the coastal waters of the Gulf of Maine. From Cape Cod to Mount Desert Island and beyond to Nova Scotia, my family and I have spent endless hours admiring its independent people, breathtaking geography and mystical call. Very few places on earth provides its stewards with more beauty, charm and majesty than the rugged coast of Maine.

My love for the sea, and strong admiration for its people who have chosen to risk their lives each day fishing its waters, has inspired me to write this story. It is a story about the constant struggle that man has with the forces of nature, and how undying love and impenetrable faith becomes his protector.

It is my belief that man grows in spirit and love when he is challenged to go beyond his own expectations, and unselfishly uses the gifts that he has been given, for the benefit of all mankind. The footprints that we leave behind are not measured in the distance along life's shore, but in the depth that they penetrate the ground that supports the life it sustains.

Jerry Flauto

Contents

Chapter One

The aging sea Captain stared out of the bay window into the boatyard where he had spent most of his life living to the rhythms of the sea. The man's silver gray hair and tan weathered face validated his time spent at sea, working the cold waters of the North Atlantic coast. The numerous islands that speckled these cold waters often reminded him of a distant place where his father had fished the warm Mediterranean waters off the southern coast of Greece and the Aegean Sea. But this was not Greece; it was the region along the North Atlantic coast, called "New England."

The name, "New England," was derived from those who first settled upon a new land, which offered them freedom from oppression. These brave people who risked their lives to travel on small boat's across the mysterious and often dangerous Atlantic Ocean were seeking a "new place" where they could live freely and honor a power greater than man. And while the reason for inhabiting this land can be explained by the historical facts surrounding their arrival, the newness of the land began eons before man arrived.

The forces of nature that formed New England and the resulting landscape that met the vast ocean called Atlantic, was steeped in beauty far beyond anything that mortals could create. Man's role would be that of a steward of the land and sea.

In return, he would be allowed to share the bounty that was spread out before him, taking from it what was necessary to sustain life and nothing more. Those who might abuse this privilege would risk the unpredictable nature of mysterious forces beneath the sea that were capable of haunting their lives forever.

This land had been formed by the awesome power of frozen glacial waters that sculpted its boundaries in ragged fashion, leaving behind masses of colored rock and steep cliffs that harmoniously blended the land and sea together. Where the land and sea met, the melting waters left behind a place where nature would flourish, and man and creatures of the sea would mingle in a constant battle for survival. Below the water's surface, these same glacial forces were known to cut deeply into the land below the sea, sometimes leaving vast open crevices that penetrated to mysterious immeasurable depths.

In a unique place, a portion of this land had been carved inward toward the west, leaving the "Gulf of Maine" in its wake. This body of water emerged as host to man and many sea creatures, because its temperature was shielded from the colder North Atlantic waters. The warm Gulf Stream flowing northward up the Atlantic coast would be drawn into the Gulf of Maine and mingle with the colder North Atlantic waters. The resulting warmer seas would be host to all forms of sea life, from simple highly enriched plankton to mammoth gray whales... and often mysterious creatures that would defy one's imagination.

Dolphins and assorted sea life up and down the food chain were the benefactors of this banquet of nature. Lobsters, shellfish, clams and sea urchins lived at the bottom of the sea, and added to the menu that man would harvest for his survival.

The Captain's reputation in Black Point Cove was one of meticulous pride, and everyone knew that his boat, the *Eagles Wing's*, was the best-kept and best running boat in the Cove. Each morning before dawn, the Captain would load lobster traps, and a barrel of fish heads or cunning purchased from the canning plant to be used as baitfish for the day's work. Before starting out to sea, the Captain always bowed his head and said a prayer to ask God to protect him and allow him to take part in whatever gifts were to be received that day. His prayer always ended by grasping a short rope attached to a ship's bell, and with a swift tug the bell was awakened with its un-mistakable sound... "Ding-ding" that sent gulls screeching into the air. He would take a brass key from the key ring attached to his belt and insert it into the keyhole on the pilothouse bulkhead. With a slight turn of his wrist, the engine immediately came alive with its unmistakable "putt-putting" sound. "Good girl," the Captain would say, and the *Eagles Wing's* was ready to take him to sea. His strong confident hands moved the gearshift lever into position, and the *Eagles Wing's* gently slid into motion, guiding the Captain safely to his destination.

At the end of each day, after returning back to the harbor, the ritual of cleaning and preparing the boat for the next day's fishing would usually take place. The Captain would grab a hose in one hand and turn on a bilge pump, which flooded the deck with fresh seawater. He then grabbed a long-handled scrub brush and labored without hesitation until the deck was clean. The remaining water was brushed overboard through scuppers beneath the rail, leaving the deck in pristine condition.

When all seemed ready, one last step followed. An ornately crafted mahogany box, finished in glossy varnish, and decorated with brass trim was opened, and a soft white cloth was removed from it. Next came out a can of *"Admiral Gold's Brass and Silver Polish."* The lid was carefully opened revealing its creamy saddle-colored contents, and gently dipping the cloth into the can, the Captain gathered just enough polish to finish the mission at hand. The Captain approached the starboard side of the pilothouse, and stretched his arm towards the saltwater spattered ship's bell.

As ship's bells go, this one was about ten inches tall... much smaller than other ship's bells, but it had a sound that surpassed any of them. By nature, the precise shape and curvature of a bell would define its sound and resonance. This bell was somehow different from all other bells and produced a sound that had never been duplicated from other bells. Upon hearing the sound of the *Eagles Wing's* bell, every fisherman in the Cove was made speechless as its intoxicating sound pealed almost endlessly over the Cove.

Deep inside, the Captain knew that the bell was somehow related to the *Eagles Wing's* soul, and so he treated it with reverence. It was appropriate for this much respect to be given to the bell, for many times it became the protector and guardian during storm-swept or fog-draped seas. Even during the loudest of thunderstorms and over the pounding crash of waves upon her deck, the bell's magical sound would pierce through the pea-soup fog, and guide the boat to safe harbor. Nothing could silence the piercing "ding-ding" sound of the bell, which spoke of peace and comfort when nothing but fear and confusion raged beyond the Ship's rail.

The Captain knew that the sound of the bell was also kin to his own spirit, and he knew that like his soul, the bell needed care to survive. With gentle and deliberate attention, the polish was released from the soft cloth, and after several minutes the bell emerged shining like gold. When the Captain looked into his hands holding the soft cloth and caressing the bell, it reminded him of the hands of God caressing his own soul when he needed restoration. When the job was completed, the Captain quickly wiped off the ornate brass trimmed box with the lingering polish left on the cloth, and then returned the can and cloth into it for the next day's revival.

The people of the Cove never could understand why the Captain still paid so much attention to the sleeping *Eagles Wing's*, now perched upon its storage cradle, waiting for another season to fish the crystal blue waters of the Cove, but no one talked much about it out of respect for the aging Captain. After all, it was he who had given so much to those seafaring men's lives so that their survival stayed intact.

The brave people who settled the land around the Cove, and fished its seas would inherit an obstinate passion for life; nurtured by their ability to overcome the many struggles that nature would offer them.

The numerous coves and inlets formed by glacial erosion

would become man's safe harbor from the ravages of the sea. They would build homes to protect themselves from the cold winter winds, and till the soil leading to the water's edge, where their boat's and nets awaited their journey out to sea.

Skilled, strong, calloused hands would build these boat's and repair the nets that fished the treacherous seas, where a banquet awaited below its crystal clear blue-gray waters. It was this land that man was being steward to, and he knew that his life was tied to its natural powers in a way that he often didn't understand.

As with all things in nature, balance is essential for its continued survival. When balance is upset, nature makes adjustments, where the stronger element may flourish and the weaker element may perish. Occasionally, natural forces will emerge to confuse its stewards, and the balance will tilt to reveal a different outcome that never before could be expected. It was this land and sea that the Captain had become a righteous steward to, and where balance had been challenged many times by nature.

Looking out from his window the Captain could see the safe harbor of Black Point Cove and the quiet boat yard that once bustled with small lobster boat's just like the *Eagles Wing's*. The Cove was a place where generations of Fishing family spent most of their lives rising each day, wondering if the sea would welcome them or challenge their instincts for survival.

The Captain had experienced these challenges often, and thanked God that he was spared the times that the power of the sea might have succeeded in the challenge.

In a small corner of the cove a quiet place where those that have been laid to rest, gravestone epitaph's often hinted of the grim details when the sea took the lives of individual men or whole Ship's.

The Captain would recall that one day as a young man, he was visiting the Cove's cemetery, where his mother and father had been laid to rest. The cemetery was situated alongside the small white, Saint Finbarr's Church where many of the Cove's inhabitants would celebrate their blessings. The Captain visited his parent's graves often, but always left the cemetery feeling lost and alone without their presence in his life. His father was also a skilled fisherman, and was his hero and confidant. He taught the Captain everything he knew about life at sea. His mother was the source of his gentleness and patience, and silently became the center of his life as a child. When he looked upon her grave, he could still feel her warm, loving embrace that she so often shared with him.

That day at the cemetery, an unheard voice led him to a remote, almost forgotten spot. Why he was drawn there he didn't know, but the gravestone that he now looked upon seemed to be beckoning to him. He remembered looking down at the worn gray headstone of a deceased, long forgotten seaman. As he looked upon the headstone, he searched for who it was that rested in the musty earth below his feet.

The gravestone letters were barely visible to the Captain because time had eroded its story. What was visible read, "Abraham Rumery, Born November 12th, 1824"... and then there was a long carved dash followed by, "Died October 10th, 1866. Below the dates was the inscription: "Ship's Master and friend to the men he served."

The Captain thought about what the relatively young forty-two-year-old man might have been like, and what he had done to gain the honorable distinction of being called, "A friend to those he served." As the Captain gazed at the stone, he could only wonder to himself; how did the seaman serve his men, and what led to his untimely death? Was he at peace when he died? What skills as a Ship's Master did he use to influence his crew into calling him, "a friend?"

The young man puzzled at how much was missing from the epitaph, and how the simple long carved dash separating the dates of birth and death held the mystery of the man's life... but would never reveal its story. As he stared at the gravestone, he realized that it could not reveal any more details about the person below it.

The more he thought about Ship's Master Rumery, the more

he realized at how few words were needed to describe this person he would never have the opportunity meet. After all, the most important thing about Abraham Rumery's life was that he was a friend, and very few things were more important than friendship.

The Captain would never forget this visit to the cemetery, as the epitaph became a constant reminder to him to be a good friend to all he would meet in his life.

Chapter Two

For men of the sea, days are long and difficult, beginning just before daybreak, when the sun would attempt to present its first rays on the eastern-most shore of the continent. It's not uncommon for the sun to be challenged by other natural forces that can obscure its warmth and luminance over the land and sea. Oftentimes the sun might not be seen for days or weeks at a time because of dense fog that comes unannounced, and makes navigation nearly impossible by veiling one's senses.

During bad weather only the most skilled seamen would venture out to challenge nature's intimidating mood. But overcoming nature's intrusion on man's livelihood is something that all seamen learn to embrace rather than give into. It is during these seemingly insurmountable moments at sea that experienced seamen rely on their instincts to help them clash with the danger... and live to talk about it. Most of the time they survive the intrusion... but occasionally the tide will turn and the power of nature sends a chilling message by taking even the most experienced seamen into its depths. Black Point Cove had its share of anguish and heartache when one or more of its inhabitants succumbed to the sea's grasp over them.

The Captain often reflected on stories of lost seamen who were good friends of the Cove, and how the losses were reluctantly accepted as life at sea went on.

The places where man settled often were named after their

founders, but sometimes named for a feature that described its geography or other trait. Black Point Cove got its name because of the color of an unusual steep rock cliff facing northeast and out toward the sea.

The view inland towards the back of the cove would reveal a vertical, black striped band of jagged rock emerging from the water and going straight up to the top of a high cliff. The prominent vertical black stripe contrasted with the silver-gray granite rock on either side of it, and made it a well know navigational feature. The early settlers were so moved with the unusual appearance of the contrasting colored rock cliff, that they named their new home, Black Point Cove.

In no time rugged fishing families and a fine fleet of fishing boat's populated the Cove. Soon thereafter, shops and pubs lined the harbor to support the fishermen, and Black Point Cove was on its way to becoming one of the safest harbors along the coast. However, the Cove's notoriety was not without controversy. Pub stories, formed by its patrons were often twisted and inflated by the consumption of rum and beer. One legend concerning the origin of the black rock scar, was that it was created when the devil Satan, fell from the sky in a burst of lightening and first touched the earth after he was cast out of heaven by the archangel, Michael. When Satan's body touched the cliff along the cove, it left behind a ragged black rock scar from the top of the cliff to an immeasurable crack in the depths below the water.

Why the rock was actually black, nobody truly knew, but its navigational features far outweighed the legend's concern, and the black rock face would become a focal point to guide their boat's to the safe harbor of the Cove.

When the fishermen were kept in port by bad weather or repairs, stories of strange events would unfold within the pubs that lined the harbor. But who knows if it was the rum or beer that would stimulate the storyteller's imagination or bend the truth behind his story?

Many anxious seamen would tell their stories about the strange creatures that only they might have encountered at sea. Respected veteran seaman, like Macias Crockett, a retired master shipwright, had spent most of his life at sea, and was a frequent visitor to one of the more popular pubs, *"The Thirsty Whale,"* often referred to as *"the Whale"* by the regulars. No one knew how old Machias Crockett was, but it didn't matter, "Crock," as his fellow seamen called him, was the person everyone went to when they needed to know something about the mysteries of the sea or shipbuilding.

Crock was small of stature, and walked with a slight limp, caused by an accident when a boat shifted from its moorings and crushed his leg. But even with his bum leg, Crock was as strong and nimble as any man half his age. He had a lively spirit, and with a twinkle in his eye and broad smile on his face, he made everyone he met feel like a friend. He was known to be as gentle as a lamb, but could be as ornery as a Billy goat when provoked. He lived life to its fullest and loved being with his friends, sharing his spirit with everyone.

Every so often Crock would amuse his pub friends, and surprisingly dance an animated jig, all the while holding a pint of ale... and never spilling a drop. It was here at "the Thirsty Whale," where Crock would tell chilling stories of how a poorly built ship might fail to handle the treacherous seas, and then disappear with all its crew. And while Crock was not an eloquent speaker, his words were taken seriously for what they were. He often finished his stories saying, "Ya gotta respect da sea... ya just gotta respect it... Der's no man alive is smarter den da sea."

No one doubted what Crock was saying because while most seamen never feared living at sea... all seamen feared dying at sea. And for the wife or family of a seaman, the anxious wait on a "Widows Watch", for their return was most agonizing... and each day, silent hugs welcomed the seamen home.

After Crock retired, he had far too much time on his hands, and spent many hours at the "the Whale", drinking rum, dancing jigs, and spinning tales of the sea.

Crock often would sit in a back corner and carve scrimshaw pieces depicting whales, dolphins or any other creature that captured his imagination. Crock was as much a part of the Cove as was its gray granite rock cliffs and steel blue waters. He was loved by his friends, and would often help them repair damaged boat's, just to have something to do. Crock would rarely have to pick up a tab at the Whale, for most of the seaman would be grateful for his help, and Crock was never thirsty when in their company.

It was common for any of the stories told at the Whale to include mysterious events that could never be challenged, explained or even understood. Seamen described how huge whales came to the surface, near or below a boat, and made them fear that the boat would be swamped. They would hear strange ghostly sounds, as whales talked to one another... sounds so frightening and eerie that they penetrated the thick planking used for the ship's hull, and kept seamen awake at night in fear of their lives.

One time, Crock told of seeing a giant beached squid, measuring over thirty feet long, and oozing black ink over the white sand. "Ya shoulda seen it... it waz biger'n uglier den anything eye'z ever seen." And while rarely did any of these creatures do harm to man or ship; the sight of them would bring awe and fear to the most courageous seamen.

Like any story, details were often exaggerated, placing the real truth somewhere between a little exaggeration and bold-faced lies. Add a little rum or stout, and a few anxious seamen; the story could take on a life of its own.

While Crock was a legend in the village, he and others like him had put Black Point Cove on the map. The village along the harbor was well known for its fine repair shop where any boat problem could be fixed... and never to worry that you would be taken advantage of, the owner was an honest and fair man in all his dealings.

The Cove was well known up and down the coast because of its once very successful fishing fleet and skilled shipwrights like Crock. Fishing and Lobstering was the livelihood of choice for many fishermen along its rocky coast, and building boat's for them provided income for the skilled shipwrights like Crock.

Fine lumber from the mature forests inland would be traded for fish and lobsters, and would become the materials used for building homes and boat's.

What was unusual about Black Point Cove was that it had once maintained its existence because of its willingness to trade goods taken from the sea for other goods manufactured inland, or down the coast. But this was becoming unusual in post war times, as the economy was seeing a boom as new jobs were being created for returning military men, jobs that were drawing families away from the treacherous life at sea.

Now, only a few inhabitants of the older generation still remained in the Cove. Rarely did tourists visit the village as they once did to buy souvenirs or stroll the small quaint harbor area to enjoy the view of the small boat's anchored there, or partake in a pint of cold Stout from one of its pubs.

For a long time, changes in the Cove seemed to occur very slowly as life went on, not too much differently from last week, last month or a decade ago. But now things were changing rapidly, and young families were feeling the call to be independent in the hustle and bustle of city life where they could have bigger houses, bigger cars and everything that would satisfy their desires, but without the dangers of sea life threatening them each day.

In contrast to this new but less intimate lifestyle, village life requires dependence on friends, and not much is necessary to satisfy ones needs. The sea provided you with what you needed, and whatever surplus there was, would be sold or traded to others for some special service or supplies. Money received from trading was used to purchase whatever else was required to sustain life. It was a simple, uncomplicated way of life that matched man with nature, in a never-ending struggle for survival. Those that chose to stay behind were anchored to the simple beauty of the land and sea, and nothing would draw them away from it.

The land along the sea in front of the Captain's house was as old as the sea itself, as endless waves and tides eroded its surface, leaving behind rippled gray platform-like steps of granite rock. Coarse, pearl-white colored veins of quartz, pinstriped the dark gray rock and traversed the slippery granite steps that patiently led a hundred feet or so to the water's edge.

The slippery weathered rock often invited inquisitive seekers to stroll along the water's edge to view its turbulent waves breaking over the rocky shore. But, every so often, an unaware visitor would be washed into the water by a rogue wave crashing over them. Most would emerge unscathed with only slight bruises and a shattered ego, but once in a while, the sea would keep one of its victims.

Farther beyond the large bay window, the Captain could see the gently swaying steel-blue waters of the North Atlantic, spilling over the rocky shoreline below. The Captain knew that the mood of the sea could be fickle and unpredictable at times, allowing man to share her pleasures only when her mood was merciful. When not in the mood, she might cloak herself in a veil of translucent fog and obscure man's view, leaving behind only the sounds of crashing waves on rock.

The Captain marveled at how, in man's cleverness, he would challenge the power of nature by building a stone lighthouse to overcome the sea's reluctance to accept his advances. The Breakers Rock Lighthouse guarding the entrance to Black Point Cove was typical of those along the New England coast, built as a long lasting symbol of caring, safety and vigilance.

The Cove's lighthouse was built on a seemingly precarious spot, but offered the greatest advantage to pierce the fog that could shroud man's view. The structure, like others along the coast, often appeared much too tall to withstand the pounding forces that strained against her slim body. But over time, and with the care of generations of Lighthouse Keepers, it would endure, and guide man home to the safety of the Cove.

Like a wise and crusty old seaman, each lighthouse had its own unique personality. The Breakers Rock Lighthouse was built taller than most lighthouses because it had to be seen in front of the rising granite cliffs that surrounded the Cove. Its body was built from silver-gray granite rocks quarried from the water's edge. But its special feature was a wide black stripe going from its base upward to its beacon. The black stone selected for the stripe was taken from the same black stone cliff where Black Point Cove got its legendary name.

When the lighthouse was built many years ago, the Cove's inhabitants protested this feature because of the foreboding legend of its grim origin. But who could argue their concern, when the news of a quarryman's death raced through the pubs?

The bleak story unfolded that as a team of quarrymen worked the water's edge below the black rock cliff, a worker was attracted to a perfectly square black stone sitting close to the water's edge. The quarryman felt that the square black stone would make a perfect cornerstone for the base of the lighthouse.

The quarryman carefully stepped toward the water's edge, and reached down to grasp the stone. What happened next, no one knows for sure, but the other workers heard the quarryman's scream for help. As they turned toward the man, they witnessed him being pulled into the water as if his hands were attached to the rock.

The last shrieking words from the distressed quarryman were, "I can't let go, and my hands are frozen to it!" ... and then he was gone. As the other quarrymen rushed to the spot where their friend had vanished below the strange, cold, ink-black, almost iridescent water, not a trace of his body could be seen.

Several weeks had passed before the body of the ill-fated quarryman washed back onto the black rock shore. The worker that found the dead man described the wretched soul in eerie detail; "His skin color was as gray as a dolphin's skin, and his eyes and mouth were wide open. Whatever he had seen before he died put the look of terror on his face. His hair was not washed down flat against his skull... but stood frozen, straight-out as if he had received an electrical shock."

The untimely death of the quarryman slowed the building of the lighthouse, as a Board of Inquiry from the "U.S. Life-

Saving Service" stationed in Bar Harbor, gathered information about the mishap. Not much new information came about from the investigation, and the mishap was finally ruled as an accident. Nonetheless, the lighthouse was eventually completed, as hushed stories of the events of that day became part of the lighthouse's legend.

In spite of the lighthouse's bizarre beginnings, each day thereafter, it provided safety and security for the Cove's inhabitants. When unannounced fog silently crept inland, the lighthouse's recognizable mechanical voice would repeatedly belch out raspy groans toward the sea, accompanied by the sound of its dull clanging iron bell, to warn lost seamen of the rocky cliffs below. Atop her crown, a shining beacon made of jewel-like prisms awaited the call to thrust its light outward. And like a mother's protective eyes watching her child... in an unbroken rhythm the beacon would search the horizon, and without hesitation, plunge her laser-like sword outward to pierce the moisture laden fog wall.

For centuries it had been this sight and sound that guided men of the sea back home to the safety of the Cove... but only if the sea allowed it.

On this day, the deep blue sky hinted that it would be a day of calm on the sea, and the lighthouse would sleep until the setting sun would awaken its brilliant crown to once again search the horizon.

Perhaps it was the soft whispering breeze, calm waters and blue sky that spoke to the Captain's soul this day, but whatever it was, it was long overdue and reluctantly accepted.

From this vantage point looking out from the bay window, the Captain searched far beyond the horizon for answers to questions that were anchored deep within his soul... much like the mysteries chiseled in stone on Ship Master Rumery's long forgotten gravestone. However, this day was different, as something deep inside his chest was tugging at his memory, whispering a message that he could not understand.

Many times before when he stood at this same window,

he knew why he had moist eyes and a tight feeling within his chest. Now, as he gazed across the sloping weathered rocks, reflecting on images of his wife and son, his eyes were dry and the hollow feeling was not there. The Captain was feeling a strange, almost forgotten peace within himself. He was struggling to try to understand what was speaking to him, as his life story began to replay in his mind as if it were yesterday.

What was different this time? What drew him to the window this day to challenge his instinct for survival that had been wrought by a life at sea, where danger was always waiting to sneak upon him and grab at his life?

Chapter Three

Those who knew him called him Pappas, but his birth name was Anastasios Christos Pappas, or "Taso" for short, if you were of Greek heritage. Many of those living in the Cove called him "Captain Pappas" out of respect for the man whose kindness and wisdom had touched so many people there.

Taso had inherited the skills of a fisherman from generations of family before him. As far back as he could remember, his family had lived their lives around and on the sea, receiving whatever gifts would be given up from its depths.

The rugged life of a fisherman is filled with danger and chance (but to Taso's belief), God's will. Risk was something that fisherman rarely took, for the sea was not patient with those who were careless. The sea was known to relinquish whatever gifts it chose to give... at its own choosing. If man decided to take these gifts out of greed, the sea might retaliate, and rebuke him.

For generations, the Pappas family followed the daily routines of a fisherman's life, never deviating from the patterns that provided the safest and most reliable outcomes. At the end of each day, the gifts obtained from the depths of the sea would be taken to the commercial seafood buyers, to be sold or traded for other items or services.

Taso could barely remember his past family history beyond his immediate family, because the Pappas family history had long been lost during the migration to the new world over a century ago. His immediate family, were the only Pappas's to settle on the New England coast. His father Demetrius, owned a small, but meticulously maintained fishing boat named *Eagles Wing's* that provided enough food and income to support his wife Marianas and little Taso.

For the Pappas family, and most other seafaring families, life on the sea brought little more than the required necessities that allowed a family to survive just beyond the reaching grasp of the hands of poverty. But a strong family bond and deep love for one another always overcame anything that challenged their survival.

The Pappas home was simple, small and cozy, built in the Cape Cod style and located just a few streets inland from the Cove. Marianas would plant daises and lupines in flower boxes hanging from its windows, and tend to a small vegetable garden containing tomato plants, cucumbers and eggplant, that would be used when preparing traditional Greek meals.

For a long time, Demetrius and little Taso worked side-by-side on the lobster boat, happily sharing lives as men of the sea. But life as Lobstermen was difficult and filled with many unplanned interruptions that were part of this work.

Most seamen began learning the trade at an early age by gaining experience from their fathers or other family members. Rarely did anyone complete schooling beyond sixth grade, for the skills required as a fisherman could not be taught in a classroom... they had to be experienced in a boat and on the water, where the forces of nature intermingled with man's presence.

In this regard, young Taso was different from many of his friends, and he did complete High School, only working on his father's boat on weekends or during summer breaks.

Because of the time spent at school, Taso spent less time on a Lobster boat than his young friends did, but he was clever and a quick learner, and amazingly far more skilled than most of them. But nonetheless, Demetrius felt strongly that an education was very important and that it would make a difference in his son's success. He also realized that learning the trade would be a way for Taso to have something to fall back on if anything went wrong.

Taso would often recall how he had learned so much from his father, and how they sang songs, told stories and laughed together while at sea.

During the most threatening times at sea, when at his father's side, an approaching gale might test their survival skills. The rough sea would pound the small boat while they searched for the safety of the Cove... listening for the groan of the foghorn to guide them home. It was then that a song or story became little Taso's hope.

Demetrius would steer the boat with his hands wrapped tightly around the wheel, attentively staring out of the pilothouse, often glancing back to little Taso to be sure that he was safe... all the time humming a lively Greek tune to calm the boy's fear. His father would continually assure him by offering, "Taso, Michael the guardian angel is in the boat with us... so we are protected no matter what the seas are doing... we'll be safe at home soon."

Demetrius would then grab at the rope attached to an ornately forged ship's bell, and ring it loudly, listening for its penetrating echo against the perilous rocks along the shore. And as always, he safely navigated the boat back home, following the echo of the bell, which would announce that firm land was close at hand. When they finally arrived at the dock, the boat would be cleaned in preparation for the next day's fishing, and before departing, the bell would be ritually rung one last time as they left for home.

On the way home, little Taso always seemed to lag his father's footsteps, searching along the way for some interesting creature or sight that always seemed to capture his attention. When he finally got close enough to home, he could see his father ahead of him, and his mother anxiously standing at the open door. As his father met his mother's awaiting embrace, Demetrius would remove something from his pocket and place it into her hands. She would follow the gesture by putting her arms around him and bury her head into his chest. Then she would lift her head up to plant a welcoming kiss on his cheek.

Following their greeting, Demetrius would step inside the house, and Marianas would look toward her son, crouch down with her arms wide open and beckon to him, "My little sea urchin, do not make your mother wait a minute longer, for I have missed you so much that my heart needs your love." This was little Taso's signal to run into his mother's outstretched arms... the embrace lasting much longer than any small child could endure.

"Mama," he would begin... and then a long story would unfold as to what he and his Papa had done on the boat that day. She listened attentively, her eyes fixed directly into child's eyes, as if she were on the boat with the two fishermen, as the child told every detail of the day's events. When he was finished, she would kiss him like she did Demetrius, and tell Taso, "Now let us go inside to eat... and don't forget to change your clothes and wash your hands before you come to the table."

Later that evening while sitting with his mother and father alongside the fireplace that sent warm flickering light into the room, little Taso's curiosity would not let go of his father's earlier comments about an angel on the boat. With an inquisitive tone to his voice, Taso asked his father, "Papa, who is the angel Michael, and why is he on our boat to protect us?" Demetrius smiled at the child and glanced at Marianas, whose eyes rolled upward as she silently shook her head from side to side; hinting in non-verbal fashion of what she knew was about to be explained.

Demetrius was a wonderful storyteller by nature, and any opportunity to tell one was never passed. So, a story began to unfold, telling of the angel that shared the boat with them that afternoon.

"My son," he began, "Before the curse of time was given to man, Adam and Eve were placed in the Garden of Eden... a gift given to man from God. It was a place filled with every imaginable creature, flower and food that would delight man's needs and pleasures. But before man was placed in

Eden, there was a falling out of some of the angels in heaven."

"Lucifer, one of the most beautiful angels in heaven thought that he was better than all of the others. The form that Lucifer had was one of beauty and majesty. His voice was purer than any sound ever made, and was so soothing that anyone hearing it would be lulled into a trance-like state until his voice went silent."

"Lucifer's pride led him to believe that he was better than anything in creation, and he began to think that he was even better than the Creator himself. This displeased God very much, and as a result, God directed his most trusting and obedient Archangel Michael to battle Lucifer and his followers. Michael was the only angel in heaven that could ignore Lucifer's beauty and intoxicating voice."

"God provided a special sword to Michael, which was created with all of the same elements that were used to create the earth. The sword shined brightly with fire and light, and was stronger than anything that existed. It was so strong and powerful, that it could penetrate the impenetrable."

"So, with his sword in hand, a fierce battle took place, and Michael bravely fought Lucifer and his followers. Good overcame evil and Michael won the battle, forcing Lucifer and his followers away from Heaven in a bolt of lightning that silenced the voice of Lucifer.

"When Lucifer arrived on earth, God allowed him to roam its land and seas where he took on the new name Satan, and chose the sea to live in because there was more water than land on the Earth."

"When the Garden of Eden was created, God knew that Satan would be jealous of Adam and Eve, and all of the good that was in it. So, He directed Michael to guard the Garden from Satan's return, and Adam and Eve would have Michael to protect them from his evil forces."

"Satan was crafty, sly, devious and jealous of Adam and Eve, and felt that the Earth was his alone to use as he wished. He envied everything that was in the Garden, and was determined to enter into it and take whatever he wanted. Michael was always on the lookout for Satan and expected him to appear just as he did when he was in the form of the beautiful Lucifer, with his beauty and intoxicating voice. But the sly Satan would slip past Michael because of his deviousness. Satan was able to do this because on Earth he took on the form of a giant sea creature."

'The creature was dark in appearance, and silent in its movements, turning the waters around it cold, thick and an iridescent ink-black as it moved about. Satan would never reveal his once intoxicating voice, but often would frighten other sea creatures, making eerie whale-like sounds to confuse them, often to the point that they would beach themselves on the shore and die. Wherever he roamed the sea, the foaming ink-black waters around him would turn bitter ice cold, even if the warm sun shined brightly above."

Satan's form was very different than what Michael was expecting to see as he guarded the gates to Eden. So, in his craftiness, Satan slithered out of the waters of the ocean, and changed into the form of a serpent, creeping close to the ground so that he would be less likely to be seen, and blend in with all of the other creatures in Eden."

"Satan then deceived Adam and Eve and they fell from the grace of God, and were sent out of the Garden to toil the land and experience the pain and sorrow that humans would bear until the end of time. But God knew that man would want to try to go back into Eden, so He stationed Michael on Earth to keep them from entering. It is said that as Michael guarded Eden with his fiery sword, he watched with pity as man struggled with the land to grow food for his offspring.'

"Michael was so troubled that Satan had slipped past him, that he wanted to help man in his wretchedness. So, he gave up his sword, and turned it into an earth-piercing plow blade and taught man how to break the hard clumps of earth. And while man still needed to toil the earth, he now had a tool that would help him to grow enough food for the survival of his children. Michael's compassion for man's struggle to fight the forces of evil, led him to vow to God that he would continue to help defend man and his decendants from the evil of Satan."

"The plow blade, which was once Michael's sword, was handed down from generation to generation, breaking up the most impenetrable soil so that man could grow food for survival. As man roamed farther from the land outside of where the Garden was, he eventually ended up at the edge of the sea, near Greece. There, he discovered that the sea could be fished, and he abandoned the plow for nets and boat's to catch fish to feed his families."

"The spot where the plow blade eventually ended its journey along the sea began to be covered with sand. As time passed, small thorny stems emerged from the ground around the plow blade, and fragrant Sea Roses sprouted on the vines, and completely covered it."

"It is said that nowhere else would these special roses grow, except along the sea, as a reminder of the place where Michael's sword, now a plow blade, found its rest. These same sea roses still grow only within a short distance from the sea, where it is known that their fragrance can calm the soul of any who take the time to smell them."

"Many thousands of years had elapsed when one day a poor young fisherman, who was a devout man of God, was unable to fish because of a fierce storm at sea. He walked to the edge of the water as the storm was subsiding and noticed a beautiful patch of fragrant sea roses. Not wanting to pass the opportunity to smell the roses, he bent his head low to catch their beauty and smell their fragrance."

"While taking in the intoxicating fragrance and feeling peace and calmness overtake his body, he spotted something deep within the patch of roses. Taking a small knife from his belt, he began to cut away some of the thorny vines covering the object. What finally appeared was a shiny wedge-shaped form protruding out from the sand."

"The fisherman continued to remove the sand and vine from

around the mysterious object, and lo and behold, it finally was uncovered. The plow blade that Michael gave to Adam and his decedents to pierce the earth and help them in their misery, had been revealed. The surprised fisherman was drawn to the shiny object; pulling it free from the sand and wiping it clean with his tattered coat."

"The fisherman recognized the shape to be that of a plow blade, but was puzzled as to why it shined so brightly. After all, an old buried piece of metal should be dull gray and well worn... but this blade looked new and untouched. The fisherman didn't know what he would do with plow blade, so he took it home where he placed it in a shack used for storing nets and ropes."

"Time had passed, and one day the poor fisherman had a very good catch of fish... more than he and his family could use. The poor fisherman had a friend named Megadar who was a forge master who had little work to do because of the poorness of the village. Knowing that the almost starving forge master and his family would welcome the fish, he decided to share his blessing with them."

"The fisherman took some fish to Megadar at the forge. The grateful forge master thanked him, asking if there was something he could do in return for the blessing that he had just given to him and his family. The fisherman was not interested in taking anything from the forge master because he knew that whatever gifts were taken from the sea were gifts from God."

"The fisherman knew that taking something that came freely from God, and not sharing it with others in need would be wrong. But Megadar persisted, and eventually the fisherman remembered the mysterious object found buried deep within the sea roses and sand along the sea. He commented to the forge master that perhaps he could make something from the object he found in the sand, and said that the next time he visited he would bring it to him."

"Days later, the fisherman once again arrived at the forge with some fish, but this time he also had a strange object in his hands. Megadar recognized the object and told the fisherman that it appeared to be the blade of a plow, but he had never seen the type of metal that it was made from. Megadar became very intrigued with the strange blade, and asked the fisherman if he could try to melt it and form it into some other shape. The fisherman agreed, and for many days and weeks to follow, the forge master tried to melt the blade, but was unsuccessful. No matter how hot he prepared his crucible fire, the most intense heat could not deform the blade."

"Time had passed once again, when the fisherman visited the forge master, again bringing fish for Megadar and his family to eat. When he entered the forge, he could see an intense fire blasting against a large crucible hanging from a cross brace with a handle used to help pour its contents into a mold, if it were placed below it."

"Within the crucible was the blade, as Megadar looked on in confusion, sadly proclaiming his disappointment in not being able to melt it. The fisherman shared the disappointment and offered in vow-like fashion, "If you had been successful in melting the blade; perhaps into the shape of a bell for my boat, I would use the bell to proclaim God's peace and harmony among all of God's creatures."

"Then... miraculously, at the very moment that the fisherman finished saying the words, [I would use the bell to proclaim God's peace and harmony among all of God's creatures] a strange turn of events happened. The crucible began to tremble, and the blade within it took on the appearance of being on fire, while a rainbow of multi-colored sparks spewed outward from it in all directions. Then, the plow blade slowly began to soften into a radiant, silver-gold colored liquid."

"Quickly Megadar rushed to a shelf where various molds were stored. He frantically searched the shelf and reached behind a large old mold, toppling it to the ground, but revealing a dust covered smaller one behind it. He grabbed the small mold and told the fisherman that he had never used this mold before, but that it was a small bell mold that would have been used to accompany larger bells in a church."

"Megadar rushed back to the crucible where the blade had now completely melted, and without hesitation he placed the bell mold in a position below the crucible and began to pour the radiant liquid into it."

"Immediately, silver and gold colored smoke spewed from the mold vents, followed by the fragrant smell of Sea Roses. The forge master was stunned at the color and smell, which normally would be a gray-black metallic color, followed by the dank pungent smell of burning oil used as a mold release. It was all that the forge master could do to control the flow of the precious molten liquid, only spilling a small drop onto the mold's surface, where it settled as a perfect flat circle about the size of a small coin."

"It took several hours for the mold to cool down to the point where its contents could be released... all the while the fisherman and Megadar looking on in silence... as if the mold itself were about to speak."

"Then, the time arrived for the mold to be opened. Megadar approached the mold and carefully began to disassemble its halves. When the halves finally parted, intense heat and sparks forced him away from the mold as it separated. Out of the mold came the bell, followed by the fragrant smell of Sea Roses. What finally appeared lying next to the charred bell mold, took the breath away from its onlookers. Nothing so beautiful had ever been created by man."

"The bell emerged in perfect shape... about ten inches tall with gently curved sides ending at the bell's rim. At the top of the bell was a ringed loop, where it would dangle from a support, and reveal its sound. Its proportions and shape were in perfect harmony with its ability to ring clear and true. Molded on the surface of the bell were finely detailed images of a small child, peacefully sitting in harmony among all of the creatures of the earth."

"Along the bottom rim of the bell, were delicately molded images of angels, each one different, standing wing-tip to wing-tip, in a never-ending circle. Just above the rim of angels were the words, "Let the peaceful sounds of man and nature never be silenced." The bell clapper, which was also formed within the same mold, was in the shape of an elongated teardrop, with its end revealing the molded image of a woven crown of thorns. The bell that emerged from the mold shined brightly and reflected light like no other object ever created."

"Megadar looked on in disbelief, and proclaimed in amazement that he alone had crafted the bell mold that had been removed from the shelf, and it was not created with those beautiful images and words, or even a bell clapper that the newly formed bell had."

"Both the fisherman and Megadar turned their attention to the warm smoking gray mold lying on the floor alongside of "Michael's Bell." They could see the inner shape of the old bell mold, having a different, simple straight-sided form with no sloping curve. The bell mold lying next to the emerged bell was much smaller than the ten or so inches of Michael's Bell. There were no images or words of any kind within the small mold's surfaces, and no clapper indentation was present... just as the forge master had proclaimed."

"The two men watched in amazement as the fire in the forge continued its loud roaring blast against an empty crucible, filling the room with heat and smoke. The excitement at seeing the beautiful bell overshadowed the uncomfortable heat and almost noxious smell of smoke that occupied the forge. After a while, Megadar lifted the bell from the ground and attached the clapper to it, hanging it from a low-lying crossbeam in the forge."

"A short rope was attached to the clapper while Megadar stood back, looking at his friend the fisherman, and instructed him, "Go ahead and ring it, for mankind has waited too long for peace and harmony to come to it." At that, the fisherman slowly reached for the rope, pausing for a moment... and then pulled down sharply."

"The bell instantly came alive with a sound that was like no other ever herd. The sound resonated in full tone for a very long time, far longer than any bell or musical instrument could. The intoxicating tone that emerged, penetrated the souls of the men standing near, and rapture overtook their spirits."

"Accompanying the sound of the bell, the fisherman and Megadar sensed the smell of fragrant Sea Roses, the same smell that had emerged from the mold when the bell was released. It seemed like minutes before the bell silenced, but during the bell's pealing resonation, the two onlooker's attention was mystically drawn completely to its sound."

"The sound that entered their ears immediately put the men at rest, as the feeling of peace and harmony entered their souls. The peaceful state that settled within them brought an awareness of the good that man could bring to one another and to nature. They both felt a child-like innocence come over them, as if they were playing in the carefree protection of a loving guardian."

"When the sound finally silenced, the men realized the intoxicating affect that the bell had on them, and laughed excitedly. "Once more," Megadar begged, and the fisherman pulled the rope, again filling the noisy room and their souls with the sound and feeling of peace and harmony. As the bell pealed out its mystical sound, no other sound could be heard over it, not even the blasting forge."

"Only when the bell stopped resonating, could the two men hear the other sounds within the room, and once again the smell of Sea Roses lingered within the space. As the bell silenced, the thoughts that preceded its sound became apparent to the men as they looked on in astonishment."

"The humble fisherman reverently fell to his knees as he looked up to the ceiling of the forge, as if heaven itself were opened to his eyes, and he spoke, "I do not know why this has happened to me, a poor fisherman... surely there are others who are more worthy to receive this special gift. If it is your will for me to be the steward of this blessing, it will be used for all mankind to help bring peace and harmony to him. I will place the bell on my small boat, and ring it in honor of all of the good that mankind can share with one another. Let its sound ring clear and true to all who hear it, and let their souls emerge clear and true to you."

"For the fisherman, the bell placed on his boat would become an endearing symbol of peace for him and the entire fishing village. Each day thereafter, the fisherman would ring the bell before he left the harbor and then again after he returned safely home. Everyone that heard it would be protected from the dangers that could confront them at sea, and their prosperity flourished as peace and harmony settled upon the small obscure fishing village."

"From generation to generation, the descendants of the fisherman handed down the bell, where it was cared for and moved from boat to boat, traveling throughout the world. No one knows for sure where the bell ended up, but somewhere on a small fishing boat, a humble fisherman rings its sound each day in honor of peace and harmony among man."

"As for Megadar who had helped his friend the fisherman create the bell, he was blessed with an abundance of work that lifted him and his family from poverty. The small circular coin-like remnant that escaped the bell mold was given to Megadar as a reminder of God's blessings on them. Generations of Megadar's decedents became master bell makers for all of the finest churches and cathedrals in the world."

"So my son, the bell cast from the plow blade that Michael the Archangel gave to man to help him confront the harshness of the earth, had now found its way to the sea, and into the souls of all fishermen."

Demetrius had reached the end of his story, as young Taso looked on in a trance-like state; eyes and mouth wide open as he stared at his father. Demetrius concluded, "So you see, Taso... Michael and his angels are always present where evil might befall man. He not only protects us when we are on the boat, but anytime and anywhere we trust in him and ask for his help."

Little Taso was always amazed at his father's stories, and never knew how much of the story was real, or what was made-up. Whatever the case might be, the stories did pass the time and he would learn valuable lessons from them that would follow him throughout his life.

No matter what, Taso loved his father and knew that he was always safe in his presence. Even after his parent's deaths he would feel their presence when he most needed guidance. All that he would have to do was just think of their love for him, and trust that the faithful angel would be close by.

Chapter Four

$\mathcal{Y}$ears passed as young Taso grew into a man, following the footsteps of his father as a fisherman. But now it seemed almost disheartening to Taso that he didn't think of his father and mother as often as he had done before. His parents had lived long and respected lives, his mother passing on first, followed a few years later by his father. He would continue to live in the small house that he had grown up in, and would inherit the boat in which he and his father had fished for many years.

The *Eagles Wing's* was a fine boat, well made and meticulously cared for by Demetrius and Taso. It was an early version of a traditional, wood hull, built-down design Lobster boat. Its low-to-the-water design allowed it to glide smoothly through any seas, as its single-piston engine, putt-putted effortlessly, pushing the boat through the water.

The boat was painted in unusually bright colors, typical for boat's sailing the warm waters of the Mediterranean, but it seemed out of place in the cold steel blue waters of the North Atlantic. After all, Mainers never showed their colors outwardly, whether it be their boat's or personal characters... even though their colors ran deep within their private souls. The *Eagles Wing's* was painted in bright red, yellow and silver colors, and was easily recognized as "Captain Pappas's" boat by any of the fishermen of the Cove. A red canvas mizzen sail hung from a short mast attached to the stern, where it would capture even the smallest breeze and silently propel the boat forward when the engine was not in use. The wind was a gift from God, and Taso knew that using it instead of his motor would be a wise thing to do.

The contrasting cold salty sea and penetrating rays of the sun could cause much wear on a boat and its crew, but Taso was proud of the boat and continued to care for it as his father had taught him to. Taso never missed doing maintenance, and kept the brass fittings and an ornate bell hanging on the wheelhouse brightly polished. The boat always looked as if it had just been built, and stood out, among the other fishing boat's in the Cove.

Wise fishermen know that if you're going to be successful and want to stay alive, you needed to have four things: a good boat; a good motor; good gear and a lot of ambition. Taso the fisherman had all of the above and was well regarded among his friends, knowing that they could depend on him and his boat if ever they needed help.

Taso had learned his seafaring skills from the best fisherman in the Cove, his father... and he too become a respected seaman and friend to the other Lobstermen.

Using his knowledge and wisdom, he pointed out to the other Lobstermen that if they pooled their catch and stored it in under water pens until the prices were more advantageous, they would all be more profitable. This scheme worked, and soon thereafter, the "Black Point Cove Co-op" was formed... and the Lobstermen were more profitable than ever before. Besides, any scheme that made the Lobstermen work closer together made them more stable and brought harmony to the Cove.

Taso was also regarded as a peacemaker, and well respected for his wisdom in matters that involved difficult issues.

The Black Point Cove Co-op participants often fought over where their individual traps would be placed during the fishing season. If one fisherman was catching more fish than another, suspicion surfaced and arguments would ensue. To quell the arguments, Taso proposed that each person would have a permanent area to set traps, and an open area where anyone could place traps. While the scheme was not perfect, it helped keep balance and some semblance of order in the Cove.

Taso was also somewhat of a legend in the Cove because of the time he rescued a fisherman in distress... some saying that he actually saved the man's life. It happened on a cold wind swept day when Taso was fishing alone, off the waters of "Praying Rock," a place that got its name from a sheer rock formation resembling hands folded in prayer. While fishing there, he was somewhat aware of a small white lobster boat working the waters a hundred or so yards away. But suddenly while tending one of his own traps, he was startled by a distant sound that seemed to be a man screaming in pain. He looked across the water toward the sound, and could see the small white boat, but could not see anyone on it. Seamen are known for their concern for one another, and the call to respond preempted everything that Taso was doing.

Taso immediately dropped his trap, unaware that it held an abundance of lobsters. He started his engine and turned the boat to the starboard direction, full throttle ahead as the boat pushed toward the small white boat. As the brightly colored *Eagles Wing's* approached the distressed boat, Taso decided to signal his advancement by pulling on the rope attached to the boat's bell. The bell came alive, sending a long lasting resonating sound across the water... a sound that would drown out the motors full throttle groan. A quick moment passed as Taso's eyes held fixed on the small white boat. At once he could see a bloodied arm rise above the distressed boat's rail.

Taso now sensed the worst, as he stopped his motor and settled alongside the white boat. Instinctively he grabbed a line and secured it to a cleat from his boat to the other boat, and peered over the rail to see what was there.

He now could see a man lying on the deck, whose blood soaked arm was tangled within a mass of twisted rope. "Help me!" The man pleaded, as Taso observed a tangled rope going from the man's arm to the deck below a spinning pot hauler pulley, also spattered with blood. Taso knew right away what had happened, for a pot hauler's pulley was notorious for snagging its operator.

Taso grabbed for his belt knife and cut the rope loose from the injured man's arm. As the man's twisted arm fell limp to the deck. He feared the worst, expecting to see the man's arm torn loose from his torso, but the man's coat concealed it.

Taso quickly fell to his knees alongside the man, and began to remove the blood stained coat. To his relief, the arm was still attached, but twisted in an unnatural position. The rope had cut deeply into the man's shoulder, exposing muscle and bone... but it was still intact.

"What's your name fella?" Taso offered in a gentle tone, not wanting to frighten the man any further.

"Shawn... Shawn Foster," the man responded.

"Well Shawn, you're going to be okay, but first we have to stop this bleeding." Shawn looked toward his shoulder and silently cringed at the site. Taso removed the jacket he was wearing, and then his shirt... oblivious to the unusually cold air that surrounded the boat. He placed his shirt over the exposed arm, tucking it under Shawn's armpit and then tied it in place with a piece of rope.

"Well Shawn, that should stop the bleeding for now... is there anything else that might be broken, besides your spirit?" Shawn responded, lifting his back from the deck and saying, "I don't think so... it happened so fast and all, I was just dragged to the pot hauler before I knew it. My arm jammed into the pot hauler's pulley and the pain just overcame my body. I don't remember much after that; I think I blacked out... but I just don't remember much more than that... except, I do remember hearing the sound of a bell... yes, I heard a bell ringing, and the pot hauler immediately released my arm... and I ended up here on the deck." Then Shawn's body sank back onto the deck, as weakness seemed to overtake his consciousness.

Taso knew that he had to get him to a hospital quickly,

before he lost too much blood, and asked, "Do you think you can make it back to shore if I tug your boat back to the Cove?" Shawn answered, "Yes, I think I can make it." Taso instructed him to lie down on the deck and not move. "If you need something, just raise your good hand and I'll stop, and come back to you... got it?" Shawn raised a thumb and laid his head on a makeshift pillow made from Taso's coat. Then, the bare-chested Taso tied the white boat to the *Eagles Wing*'s and proceeded to tug it to the Cove.

When the boat came within sight of the dock, he rang the ship's bell once again to get the attention of the dockworkers. The bell's sound, and the sight of the *Eagles Wing*'s towing the white boat, and the bare-chested Taso in his pilothouse got everyone's attention on the dock.

When the boat finally arrived at the dock, everyone standing there went into action, leaping onto Shawn's boat and retrieving the injured seaman. Shawn was placed on a stretcher and was ushered to the landing where an ambulance would soon take him to Grace Memorial Hospital, only a short drive away.

While waiting for the ambulance, Shawn told of the heroics of the man who saved his life, and how the sound of a bell seemed to speak to the pulley, demanding that it release him.

Looking in the direction of Taso, Shawn repeated, "I'm alive because of that man and his boat. In a minute my arm could have been used for baiting my traps," But Taso knew that this was no cause for celebration, for he was sure that Shawn's career as a fisherman would be short lived, and his arm would never again be able to lift the heavy traps that provided a living for him and his family.

This day, the sea would not claim victory over man, but the scars left behind would be a constant reminder of the battle.

Chapter Five

The years had passed since the incident on the small white boat, and the waters of Black Point Cove showed very few signs of the once flurried activity that the fishermen acted out each day. Then one day while Taso was gazing out from his familiar bay window overlooking the Cove, his thoughts shifted, as they often did, to the one person who had stirred the deepest parts of his soul. She was the woman who shared his love and gave him the most precious gifts, love and life itself.

Alexandra Savallas was her name, and she had within her a spirit that was filled with passion, love and kindness beyond what any other woman possessed. To look upon her, one would see a gentle figure of a woman, with smooth olive colored skin and long flowing silk-like black hair that draped over her shoulders and flowed down her back. Her almond-shaped dark brown eyes sent sparkling light outward like the beacon atop a lighthouse, while her face seemed to draw one into her presence.

Her Greek heritage had been interrupted a generation ago when she left the small island of Ikaria on the eastern coast of Greece in the Aegean Sea, and headed for nursing school in America. And while she still had family in Greece, she was at home in New England where fishing and a love for the sea was a constant reminder of her island heritage.

Alexandra possessed a smile that evoked trust, and in her company everyone felt comfort and confidence. Her presence seemed to light up a room, as she moved with grace and charm among her friends. In any other place, she would be mistaken as royalty, but among those less privileged of Black Point Cove... she was just Alexandra.

She too, like Taso was an only child, and had experienced the grief of losing both parents far too soon for a young woman. But she endured life by clutching onto her faith while working as a nurse at the nearby Grace Memorial Hospital in Jonesport. At the Hospital, she was regarded as one of the most well liked and compassionate nurses, often volunteering free time to comfort the most critically ill patients.

When not working at the hospital, she spent time at Saint Finbarr's Church on the hill overlooking the cove, where she organized a food pantry to help the poorest of the cove's inhabitants.

She gained the reputation of being a fine cook, and would prepare special dinners for those less fortunate, quietly delivering the meals in a linen covered basket, always with a fresh flower laid across its top.

Wherever she was, and whatever she did, those who were in her presence felt her energy and passion for life, and were moved to share their gifts with one another... as she so often did with them.

It was in the autumn of 1946 when Taso first met Alexandra at a community gathering in Saint Finbarr's gathering hall, honoring returning military men who had served in the war. Taso was one of the guests who would be attending the gathering, after spending several years in the Navy. He had left the cove four years earlier, and was not knowledgeable in the strange ways of the world. But that would change, as he would experience the hell of war, as his ship was under attack by German U-Boat's.

While Taso was never injured during these attacks, he had witnessed death and suffering when a torpedo struck the hull of his ship, igniting fuel and munitions below deck. He received the "Navy Cross" medal for saving several of his shipmates...

rushing to their aide below deck as fuel oil exploded and the ship burned.

The men that he pulled from the fiery hell below would have another chance at life, their faces and limbs forever scarred from the battle, a constant reminder of the war. Taso always shied away from accepting any praise for what he did that day, always saying, "I just did what anyone else would have done." Now, he would try to put the pain of war behind him, and start life all over again.

Taso had been reluctant to go to the gathering, realizing that he wasn't the same person that had left the Cove years ago... not sure that anyone would recognize him. He was also worried that he might not recognize anyone there, for time had passed and many of his fishermen friends had left the Cove for other places. But eventually, reason overcame reluctance, and he decided to go to the celebration... after all, there were old friends to greet and new ones to meet.

The day finally came, and he dressed in his neatly pressed uniform, looking into his mirror and placing his sailor hat on his head. He smiled at what he saw and tilted his hat slightly forward and winked. Then he lifted his hand to his forehead in a final salute to the man in the mirror. He was now on his way out, after all, the gathering awaited his presence.

The short walk from his house took him along an elevated pathway that separated the sea from the land. He passed a long rectangular granite rock that was shaped like a bench, and was lying on a strategic spot overlooking the ocean. He recalled that as a boy, he and his mother often spent hours together sitting on the rock and talking, while looking out to sea where Demetrius was fishing somewhere beyond their sight. This was his special place, and he paused for a moment, and was sure that he sensed the spirits of his parents as he passed by.

A few hundred yards away as the path gently turned inland away from the sea, he could see the Church with its small gathering hall, built on a similar spot having an equally commanding view of the ocean. As Taso approached the church, he could hear sounds coming from a side door leading to the gathering hall. "Well, here goes," he whispered to himself as he entered the door and was now in the presence of the people of Black Point Cove. He thought to himself that it might have been easier to rush into a burning ship than where he had just entered, for he was basically a shy man and not normally the one to introduce himself to others. He cautiously entered the hall and immediately could feel heat build up under his uniform, and on his forehead, where unseen beads of sweat were poised for exposing themselves.

As he glanced to the opposite side of the room, he was drawn to someone whom he didn't know... but before the end of the evening, would share his soul with. Something special seemed to radiate from her presence. Perhaps it was her long dark hair and sleek figure, or maybe the grace at which she moved from table to table talking to the guests. Her laugh could be heard softly above the sounds within the room, and like others, Taso was immediately drawn to her presence.

Alexandra's smile was infectious, and awakened feelings of welcome and peace to the man who had experienced the loneliness and confusion of war. As Alexandra glanced back toward Taso, she too was drawn to his presence and politely ended her conversation with one of the other guests.

Alexandra's job that evening was to greet the guests, and without hesitation she moved toward the door where Taso stood staring into the room, not sure of what he should be doing. As she approached Taso, her hand extended to greet him and her smile preceded her words of welcome. "Hello Sir! I'm Alexandra, and my friends call me Alex... and we're honored that you've come to our celebration."

Her soft hand met Taso's, and for a moment he didn't know what to say, for he was stunned by her presence and greeting. Then in rapid-fire fashion he spewed out, "Why, ah... oh, yes... I'm glad to be back in Black Point Cove, it's been a few years since I left... my name is Anastasios Christos Pappas... and I'm the only son of Demetrius and Marianas Pappas who lived and fished here in the Cove for many years before their deaths... I'm also a fisherman, at least that's what I did before

I enlisted in the Navy, where I served on the *USS Preble* as a mechanic... in the Atlantic fleet.

Then, Taso abruptly stopped talking, as he realized that his uniform made it clear that he served in the Navy, and of course he must be a fisherman... why else would anyone live in the Cove. He quickly thought that perhaps he was talking too much, about too many things that Alexandra might not be interested in. Then he offered, "But most people call me Pappas."

Slowly and gently the handshake continued unbroken, as they stared into each other's eyes. "Well then," Alexandra replied, breaking the spell, "Pappas it'll be, for we are now friends, and so you must call me Alex."

Taso felt relief, as they continued their handshake until they both realized that the formality of the greeting had ended moments earlier... both being reluctant to release each other's hand. When they realized what was happening, their faces showed a blush, and Alexandra broke the tense moment with a confident smile, saying, "Please come in and I'll introduce you to more friends." Their hands slowly slipped from one another's, as Alexandra looped her arm through his and led him into the room to re-introduce Taso to the friends of Black Point Cove.

At each table she would introduce Taso, "My friends, I would like you to meet Anastasios Christos Pappas, whose parents were Demetrius and Marianas Pappas... longtime residents and friends of the Cove, perhaps you might have known them? Mr. Pappas served in the Navy, on the *USS Preble*, to help protect us from harm. All of his friends call him Pappas, so we too shall call him Pappas."

Friends at each table stood to greet Taso, shaking his hand and saying "Nice to meet you Mr. Pappas... or, can I call you Pappas?" "Yes, of course, call me Pappas" he would reply, as he was astounded at how Alexandra had introduced him and his family with such honor... remembering their names and everything he had briefly shared with her moments before. Alexandra was speaking as if she and Taso were old friends, and the people that he was introduced to that evening openly welcomed him as one of their friends.

As the evening progressed, Alexandra led Taso from table to table, and he began to relax, feeling very much a part of the place that he had left several years ago. He was realizing that this was his home and he belonged to it, rather than it belonging to him.

Then, at one particular table while Alexandra was again introducing Taso to other guests, but before she had time to finish the introduction, a man sitting at the opposite side of the table abruptly stood up and spoke in a loud excited manner;

"I know you... you saved my life, remember me, I'm Shawn... Shawn Foster."

At first Taso didn't recognize the man, but then, the image of a small white boat entered his mind, and of course he recognized Shawn. "Yes" Taso blurted as he quickly stepped around the table and placed both of his hands on Shawn's shoulders, and with just as much excitement he answered, "You're okay aren't you? The last that I remember seeing you, you were being taken away to the hospital... and that arm, how is it?"

Taso glanced to Shawn's left arm that seemed to droop in an awkward position, with his hand turned strangely inward. Shawn smiled and said, "Well, it's not like it was before the accident, but if you hadn't come along when you did, I'm sure that I would have lost it completely. It works to some extent, but not good enough for me to fish anymore. So, I changed careers and have a repair shop down by the dock, where I can make a fair living fixing boat's... and besides, with my wife's baking, we're doing okay."

Then Shawn turned to his side and looked down at the bright smile of a woman who was absorbing all that was being said. "Oh, I'm sorry Mr. Pappas, this is my wife Megan, and what I said was true. I'm not sure if my customers come to my shop for the repairs, or the bread and cookies she makes."

As Megan was being introduced to Taso, she stood up and politely reached out her hand toward him.

Megan was tall and slender, with light sandy-colored hair that was more brown than blond. Then she gratefully offered, "Mr. Pappas, I must thank you for what you did that day to save my husband's life. If you hadn't been there, we wouldn't be here today. My Shawn is the best guy in the world, and has made my life wonderful, and I'm very grateful that you gave him a second chance."

Taso was embarrassed at all the attention, and replied in somewhat of an apologetic manner. "No, no, don't even say that... what happened that day was an accident, and anyone would have helped. I didn't do anything special."

Shawn sensed Taso's discomfort at the notoriety, and broke the tension by saying, "Please Mr. Pappas, sit with us and have a glass of wine... so we can get to know one another." Then looking over to Alexandra, Shawn spoke again, "Alex... would you mind, please join us, this is a special day, and we should take advantage of it."

Alexandra smiled, and replied, "Yes Shawn, this is a special day, and I'd love to join you in this celebration." At that, Taso interrupted, "Everyone, enough of this Mr. Pappas stuff, please call me Pappas."

The day would certainly become a special one for all of them, for everyone felt comfort in one another's presence, and by the end of the evening there would be no doubt that they would become best of friends. As the evening finally came to an end, the two couples walked outside of the church hall together, Megan's hand clasped in Shawn's, and Alexandra's arm looped within Taso's arm.

The clear evening sky was filled with a million stars, while the moon radiated a blue-white glow, sending moon shadows across the land leading a short distance to the sea. The sound of soft waves echoed off the granite cliffs, and added to the natural beauty of nighttime along the sea.

Without ever saying a word, the couples stopped, as if they had planned it, and looking upward, they smiled at the clear night sky. Then, to their surprise as they looked upward, a streak of blue light moved across the northeast sky, as if in slow motion, leaving a trail of stardust behind like the tail of a kite. Almost in unison they gasped with excitement, with "Oh's and excited "Aah's" as if fireworks had been released for their pleasure... and inside, they knew that this was a good sign.

Megan turned to Alexandra to finish her goodbyes, thanking her for such a great time, and offered, "I have a great idea... would you and Pappas like to come over to our house for dinner this Saturday?" Taso turned to Alexandra, almost expecting her to find an excuse not to accept the invitation, but then she glanced back, looking into his eyes, and said, "Pappas, I would love to visit with Shawn and Megan, I'm available, how about you?"

Taso answered almost too quickly, "Yes, of course, I couldn't think of anything better than to be with my new friends."

"Well it's done," Megan, said, "Shawn and I will see you both on Saturday, seven-o-clock... bye-bye."

Megan began to turn toward home, still holding Shawn's hand, but Shawn interrupted the motion, saying, "Hold-on just a second honey, I want to talk to Pappas for just a minute." Shawn turned to Taso and began to speak to him, "Pappas, I don't know what your plans are for the future, but if you need some work, I can certainly use help at my shop. Most of the time I'm so busy that I can't handle the work and have to turn a lot of it down, especially during the winter months and during the fishing season.

Taso responded, "Well Shawn, thank you for the offer," and then continued on... "I'm going to try Lobstering again, and get my boat back into the water, but there might be some time left where I can help you, let's see what happens... I appreciate your offer, it's very kind of you."

"Great," Shawn replied, "Just come down anytime you

want, and I'll show you around the place, and even more importantly, you can try some of Megan's Cinnamon Rolls, they're the best in the Northeast."

Megan smiled as she patted Shawn's belly, saying, "And you're an expert at eating them, aren't you?" At that, they all laughed and began to part for their homes.

Alexandra and Taso continued to walk a little farther along the path, when they approached the stone bench that Taso had passed earlier. "Would you like to sit a while Alex, this is one of the most beautiful spots on the cove."

Alexandra glanced at the stone bench, and then out to sea, pausing before saying, "This is beautiful... yes, and I'd love to."

This was the first time that the couple was alone, and both of them felt comfort in each other's presence. "Well Taso" Alexandra spoke softly to her new friend, as she once again placed her arm through his. "I had a wonderful time, and it's been a delight being with you... and I'm looking forward to Saturday night."

Taso was pleased that Alexandra had called him by the more intimate name, Taso... for which only a true Greek would know the personal translation of the name Anastasios. Alexandra noticed Taso's reaction to her using the name Taso, and immediately began struggling with an apology, saying, "Oh I'm sorry Pappas... I mean Anastasios, Oh no... I mean Mr. Pappas... I didn't mean to be so brash as to call you by the nickname Taso.

Taso tightened his arm around Alexandra's arm, as their bodies were drawn closer to one another, while he quickly interrupted her apology, "No, please don't be sorry, I'm very happy that you are calling me by my real name... it brings me comfort that you call me who I am. If it would be okay with you, I would like to call you Alex, as you had mentioned that your friends call you by that name... and I would like to be your friend." Alexandra blushed softly as she reacted to his comment, "Yes Taso, I would like you to be my friend, and to call me Alex, for that too is who I am."

Taso realized that he had met a very special person, one who had silently lit a fire deep within his soul. He recognized that Alexandra was as different from the other women in Black Point Cove, as he was different from the other men of the Cove. He knew that he wanted to become a close friend to her, and his response would hopefully ignite the beginning of a relationship that would be blessed by the fiery symbol of stardust falling from a shooting star moments before.

Nothing more needed to be said, as they continued to look out over the vast ocean, and began to share with one another subtle stories of their lives, revealing even more of whom they were. An hour or so later, the evening would finally come to an end as they resumed their walks home, once again stopping at a divide in the path where they would part from one another.

Taso would go in one direction, and Alex in another, both silently yearning for the moment never to end. But before they finally parted, Alex spoke one last time, "My house is that little one over there," as she pointed to a small, white cottage with its porch light shining alongside its front door, "And I must go now... goodnight Taso," she said as she faced the man that someday she would give her soul to. She paused; leaned forward, lifting herself up on her toes, and gently placed a quick kiss on the fisherman's cheek.

Alex then turned and slowly walked a few steps down the path... pausing momentarily, as she turned once more toward Taso, and smiled, resuming her final steps toward home. Taso continued to watch Alex as she entered her cottage and closed the door behind her. Moments later the porch light would go out, as if it were punctuating the end of a perfect evening.

Taso wasn't sure if it was the kiss on his cheek or Alex's smile that lit his soul that evening, but for sure, he felt that life would be different from that moment on. His hand slowly rose to his face, as his rough calloused fingertips touched the spot where the beautiful Alex had left her goodbye kiss.

As his fingertips rubbed up and down his cheek, a feeling deep within his chest awakened his spirit, and he reluctantly turned to go home.

His first steps toward home were slow and short, and then they became faster and longer… and finally he was running, taking quick long strides as if he were a sprinter approaching a finish line ahead of everyone else. When he finally arrived at his house he was surprised to be there, and almost fell trying to stop before he passed his door. His chest was pounding, not from the run, but because he was thinking about Alexandra.

That night would bring no rest for Taso or Alexandra, as they lay in their beds, thinking of one another. Like mountains approaching the edge of the sea, blending firm rock into soft water, their spirits had united in a natural harmony… and love would find a dwelling place.

As the week unfolded, neither Taso nor Alex could help but anticipate the approaching weekend when they would once again meet. Each day Taso would dream the image of Alexandra's graceful approach as he entered the gathering hall, and the feel of her arm looped into his as they moved about the hall. He would catch himself touching his cheek, where Alex had placed her goodbye kiss, dreaming for one more chance to re-live that moment. She too, would find herself thinking of the handsome young Taso, and eagerly anticipating the time when they would meet again… but perhaps this time he would be bold enough to embrace her in his strong arms and impart the kiss?

The agonizing wait finally came as Saturday arrived, and the couples met once again, as if they had never parted. Their relationship was as though they had known each other forever. From that evening on, they would become best friends and share in each other's lives.

The two couples would often spend a Saturday or Sunday together, and grow to know everything about one another. Each time they met, the gathering was celebrated with the clicking of wine glasses and a toast to their friendship and health. Both Megan and Alexandra were superb cooks, and their gatherings always included special meals prepared with the care and expertise of the finest chefs of the day. Alexandra's dishes always contained the hints of Mediterranean seasonings and were rich in taste and aroma. Megan always prepared New England style dishes such as New England Pot Roast with fresh vegetables, or various chowders made with fresh seafood and spices. Her exceptional baking skills always resulted in crusty hot breads and desserts that complemented steaming cups of fresh brewed coffee or tea. Any gathering of the couples would end with full stomachs and hours of endless conversation as they shared stories of their lives as they bonded like a close family.

Something almost spiritual seemed to knit the relationship of the couples to one another, and they knew that they would do anything to help each other if ever in need.

Taso and Alexandra's courtship had solidified their bond of love, and wherever they gathered, the sounds of laughter would punctuate their fondness for one another. When they entered a room, attention quickly turned toward them, for they always made everyone they met feel special. And as always, when it came time to part, leaving one another was met with reluctance as they agonized the time they would be apart.

Taso would always walk Alex back to her cottage, making sure that she was safe inside before leaving her. Often they paused on their journey home, sitting on the stone bench where they spent their first moments gazing out at the ocean. Alex would place her arm around Taso's waist as the cool sea breeze played across their bodies. She would place her head on his shoulder and embrace him, never wanting to part. They would spend endless hours sitting there, sharing their dreams and growing more and more in love with one another.

What began months ago, with a simple handshake at the entrance to a gathering hall... had grown into a deep, intimate love relationship. But time would always end their embrace, and they would have to leave one another for home. And as always, after taking a few steps toward home, Alex would turn one last time and smile at the fisherman before she entered her small white cottage.

The light on her porch would go dark... signaling their time apart. Then one day as the couple stopped at the special place where they had dreamed in each other's arms, Taso asked Alex to marry him... and their dreams would finally become a reality.

Chapter Six

The days following the announcement of the couple's engagement were filled with excitement as Alex and Taso spent their time together planning for their marriage. Everyone in the Cove buzzed with talk of the wedding that would occur in the spring,

They spent their time planning their wedding in between work and visiting with their friends. Taso was very busy getting the *Eagles Wing's* back into the water, and re-building traps for the fishing season that had just begun.

When not fishing, he helped Shawn in his repair shop, where many of the fishermen had projects needing attention. Shawn knew that Taso's help would make the shop successful. On the other hand, Taso really enjoyed working at the shop where his skills as a navy mechanic complimented Shawn's, and the duo became well respected in the cove.

But Taso's real love was being a lobsterman, and he often talked about the time spent on his boat, setting traps and gathering the gifts of the sea. He was proud of following in his father's footsteps, making a respectable living as a fisherman. It worked for his father, and it was working for him. Like his father, he appreciated nature and the gifts that he might be allowed to take from the waters below.

Alexandra too loved being close to the sea, and she was drawn into Taso's life as a fisherman. She loved being with him, and when she could, she would await his arrival on the dock after a day spent tending his traps. Taso would rush to clean his boat and empty it of the days catch so that he could be with Alexandra. The signal that announced the end of his workday was always the sharp "ding-ding" of the ship's bell, and then Taso would leap over the boat's rail, onto the dock where Alexandra often awaited his return.

One special day when Taso was leaving the boat after fishing all day, Alexandra greeted him. She spoke as always with loving affection, "Welcome back my love... I hope that the sea was good to you today," and she reached her arms around his waist, burying her head deep into his chest. Taso replied, "Yes Alex, the sea was good to me and my safe return is proof."

Alexandra often pleaded with Taso, "Someday take me out with you so that I could see the place where you work. My ancestors fished much the same as you do, and I miss the feel and smell of the open sea." Taso held onto Alex and answered, "Someday... perhaps someday." Then quickly Alexandra added, "Someday soon." Taso smiled back at Alexandra and ended her plea with, "Yes, someday soon my love."

Weeks and months passed while their love for one another grew deeper and deeper. Upon each return to the cove after fishing, Taso would anxiously glance toward the dock to see if Alexandra might be awaiting his arrival, as she now would often do. Then one day after returning from tending his traps, Alexandra was there once more, her smile lighting up the harbor. Taso instinctively grabbed the bell rope and sent a welcome sound pealing out from it to Alexandra. When the boat finally reached the dock, Taso secured it and once again leaped off the boat into her arms.

As they embraced one another, Taso was first to speak, "Alex, it's time for us to be together at sea. Tomorrow is Saturday, and you don't have to work at the Hospital, so you'll come with me to see where I fish... and maybe your spirit will be rekindled with your ancestors."

Alexandra replied with surprised excitement in her voice, "Oh yes, I'd like that... just being with you is enough to rekindle my spirit, but being with you on the boat will be even better." With a serious tone to his voice, Taso added, "You've got to dress warmly, because the sea can be brutal and can send a chill deep into your bones." She replied, "Of course my love... but I'm sure that your strong arms will be enough to keep any chill away."

Taso shook his head and laughed as they left the dock arm-in-arm to await the next day's adventure. For the loving couple the evening crawled on ever so slowly as the anticipation of their next meeting gripped every thought.

Taso had been preparing for the day to come and wanted it to be a lasting memory for Alexandra. He made sure that the boat was arranged as never before, and that only a few traps would be tended so that he could spend more time with Alexandra.

Alexandra was so excited that evening that she couldn't sleep because she would be at her lovers' side the next day, and not separated by the vastness of the sea and the dangers that could be present.

Early the next morning, Taso arrived on the boat to make sure that it would be perfect for the day's anticipated adventure. The signs in the sky showed light wispy clouds, tinted orange on the horizon where the warm sun would soon appear. He placed several warm blankets on the engine compartment where Alexandra would sit close to him as they ventured out to the ledge where his traps were placed.

The *Eagles Wing's* brass fittings and painted surfaces were inspected thoroughly, just as if she were to undergo an inspection like the *USS Preble* often had. The Captain then turned his attention to an ornately trimmed storage box sitting inside the pilothouse. Reaching into his pocket, he removed a soft, worn out piece of cloth, neatly folded it, and then placed it into the box. He closed the lid and patted its top, and with great respect he whispered... "I'll bring you home safely."

Taso continued to tend to the boat, and after all the preparations were done, he tugged on the rope attached to the brightly polished ship's bell... sending a loud resonating "ding-ding" sound across the Cove.

Taso smiled as gulls scattered about and flew in all directions at the piercing sound. "Yes, this'll do just fine," Taso whispered to himself as he glanced from stem to stern, making sure that all was in order.

Moments later he heard the sounds of short footsteps echoing off the wooden dock. As he turned to see what was approaching, he saw Alexandra coming toward the boat, carrying a large wicker basket covered with a crisp white linen cloth and a flower laying across its top.

She was dressed for the occasion, wearing snug blue dungarees and a loose cotton blouse over a turtleneck sweater that concealed her trim but well-conditioned body. Over her shoulders was a salt and pepper colored waist length wool jacket that would do just fine at keeping her warm at sea. A red print scarf that allowed her face to be the central focus of her presence held her dark hair back. Her smile bridged the distance between them and he could feel her presence even though they were not yet touching one another.

Her first words to Taso were, "Good morning my love... it feels like I've been away from you forever." She placed the basket on the dock and leaned toward his open arms awaiting his embrace.

Their positions were awkward as Taso stretched over the boat's rail to embrace Alexandra, who was now standing on the dock facing the Captain.

Their bodies drew toward one another to reclaim the time they were apart. But in their excitement at being in one another's arms, they momentarily lost their balance, almost sending them into the water.

Taso was strong and held tightly onto Alexandra, keeping her locked in an embrace that stabilized the awkwardness and prevented them from falling.

Realizing what had just happened, they both laughed out

loud, holding on to one another even tighter to keep their bodies in control. Then, never releasing his embrace, Taso carefully lifted Alexandra off the dock as if she were a feather, and placed her feet gently on the deck of the boat. Silence followed, and the day's adventure began with a kiss.

Taso broke the moment as he relaxed the embrace, making his voice sound unnaturally very serious... "And, are you ready to go to work with me today," as he stared into her eyes.

"Yes, of course Taso... I mean my Captain" she replied, "and I've prepared a special lunch for us."

Taso turned his attention to the basket sitting on the dock, and reached toward it. "What do we have here? He exclaimed," as Alexandra quickly responded by spanking his hand down and reaching for the basket herself.

She responded, "You must be patient my Captain, you'll see what it is when it's time," and she lifted the basket into the boat, looking around, and then placing it next to the ornately trimmed box in the pilothouse.

"Such a beautiful box to be on a fishing boat" she offered, "What's it for?"

Taso smiled and answered, "It's a special box that holds something that keeps me safe when I'm at sea."

Alexandra looked somewhat confused and followed, "Is it a secret?" Taso hesitated for a moment, and then answered, "No, it's part of my soul... and it helps me remember all that's made me who I am."

Alexandra's expression relaxed, as if his statement was enough to satisfy her question... for Alexandra was not one to dwell on things that were personal to others. At that moment, Taso sensed a need to reveal the contents of the box to Alexandra, and offered, "Would you like to know more about it?" Alexandra paused and replied, "Only if you wish to share it with me." She reached for his hands... much like the day when they first met.

Taso responded in a more serious tone, "Okay, it would be good for you to know about what keeps me safe at sea, because you'll be with me as we venture out today, and your safety is far more important than mine alone."

Taso turned toward the box, and with great respect he opened it and slowly reached into it to remove its contents. His hands emerged, holding a folded piece of gently warn, soft linen cloth. Taso momentarily stared at the cloth as if it was silently speaking to him... then he began to explain to Alexandra, its existence.

"You may find this strange, but my father made this box with his very own hands. It was sort of a gift for my mother, but it stayed here on the *Eagles Wing's* throughout his life as a fisherman. Each day when at breakfast, my mother would place a linen napkin next to his plate. Then after breakfast, before he left for the boat, he took the napkin and tucked it into his pocket and brought it to the boat with him. My father always wanted to have something with him that reminded him of my mother, who would be anxiously awaiting his safe return home. When he would get into the boat, he'd place the napkin in the box for safe storage during the day... and as long as the napkin was safe, he'd be safe.

At the end of the day, when he returned to the Cove, the last thing he did was to remove the napkin from the box, and return home to my mother. My mother always waited at the door for his return, and when they'd meet, he would place the napkin back into her hands, and I would hear him say to her, "I've come home to you... the softness of this cloth is returned for the softness of your hand."

My mother always blushed at that moment, and with moist eyes, she would teasingly push him away as if he were saying something that wasn't true. But she knew that it was true... as long as the napkin returned, my father was safe at home once again. To my mother, the contrasting feel of the soft linen napkin and my father's rough calloused hand in hers... validated his safe return, and a kiss would follow.

This worn napkin is the one that my father last used before

he died, years after retiring from fishing. Now I bring it with me each day at sea, as a reminder of my father and mother's love for one another... and I pray that it will continue to bring me home safely."

When Taso finished his story, he paused and stared quietly into the napkin, and then he lifted it to his lips... kissed it and then returned it to the box.

Alexandra looked on with loving reverence, as tears welled in her eyes... and then she replied, "How beautiful that was... your father and mother must have loved one another very much."

Taso responded... "Yes, while they rarely talked openly of their love, I knew that when my mother looked at my father, her eyes silently spoke of the depth of their love."

Then, for a brief moment, Alex and Taso continued to look into one another's eyes, as they reflected on the depth of love that they shared with each other, just as Demetrius and Marianas had.

Taso spoke again, "But enough of them, you're who my eyes gaze upon now, and my dreams are not concealed in my thoughts alone... I love you and I'll come home to you when my dreams of marrying you are fulfilled.

It was now Alexandra who blushed, as she responded by gently pushing Taso away from her, mimicking the gesture that Marianas had done to his father. They laughed together, as somehow the example of eternal love past had rekindled with their own new bond of love.

The intimacy of Demetrius and Marianas' love story became a part of the love that Taso and Alex would share as they drew toward the day they were to be married. But for now, Taso was anxious to share a new day with Alex.

As Taso turned to start the boat's motor for departure, he spoke again, "It's time to go now... we'll be guests of the sea, and the sea is not a patient host. You can sit here on this blanket where you'll be warm and comfortable... and don't forget to hold on as we move." Taso waited for Alex to settle upon the blanket, her feet not quite touching the deck, and then reached for the key, and turned it to start the motor.

The one cylinder motor came alive instantly, producing a hollow putt-putt sound, as a blast of water gushed from the exhaust behind the stern of the boat. Taso stepped over the rail and onto the dock where he released the mooring lines that held the boat secure. Then, he sprung like a gazelle back over the rail and into the boat. Looking back toward Alexandra, he said, "Are you ready?" and Alexandra looked back to him with her eyes wide open and a smile on her face... as she gestured back with a nod, "Yes."

Alex, all the while thought to herself, Taso was not only the strong, confident man she would marry... but also, he was now her Captain and protector on the boat. She watched as Taso eased the boat into gear and pressed the throttle forward, gently sending the boat away from the dock and into the calm waters of the Cove.

During the journey to the ledge where his traps were waiting, the Captain repeatedly glanced ahead of the boat to assure its bearings and then back again to Alexandra to make sure that she was all right. He quietly hummed a lively Greek tune that Alexandra recognized, and triggered a smile in response to his glances. Alexandra was enjoying the ride, evidenced by her peaceful smile and sparkling eyes.

The warm rising sun and gentle breeze brushed across Alexandra's face while her silky hair floated freely away from the direction the boat was heading. Her Captain smiled back... and instinctively guided the boat toward its destination.

Chapter Seven

Alexandra marveled at the vastness of the sea as the colorful boat pushed forward, occasionally sending a soft cool spray of water droplets over the bow. The boat seemed to be guiding itself as if it knew where it was headed... avoiding the multi-colored buoy's bobbing on the water's surface. She thought to herself as she looked out toward the waters' surface around the boat that there seemed to be far too many buoys for the number of lobstermen living in the Cove. Then Alexandra asked her captain, "Whom do all these traps belong too?"

Taso answered, "I'm allowed to have 600 traps, so I place them in groups of about 200 in different areas, which is about the most that I can tend in a day. It takes about three days for a trap to lure enough lobsters into it before it becomes effective to bring it up. So, by the end of three or four days I can tend all of my traps, and then I start all over again."

"We usually start the season in early spring by placing the traps farther from the shore where the lobsters have settled in during the winter months. As the season advances, they move closer to the shore where the warm waters along the gravel laden ledge will be host to their new offspring."

"By the time the season advances, we reverse our trap line placement farther out to sea. The mature lobsters and newly hatched fry begin to move to the protection of deeper water where they will stay all winter long. Then, next spring we start all over again, placing our traps farther out, but avoiding the steep drop off of the ledge, where we can lose a trap if it falls into a very deep crevasse. There's a lot of guesswork and luck in trying to predict where and when the lobsters will be attracted to my traps, but with a little luck and a lot of patience... I might just catch a few of them."

Alexandra shook her head in amazement as the Captain spoke of the complexity and perils of a lobsterman's life. She thought to herself, Taso must be a special man to choose this complicated and somewhat risky way to make a living... and how he has to know so much about the creatures living in the ocean, not to mention the sea itself, which could be so unpredictable. Alexandra was amazed at how the Captain's understanding and closeness to nature would mean the difference between success and failure as he worked the trap lines each day. She too wanted to feel the closeness to nature, and more importantly, the closeness to the man she loved.

The short journey to the ledge was about to end, as evidenced by the slowing down of the boat's movement forward and the quieting of the motor, as the putt-putt sound ended. Alexandra didn't realize how much noise came from the sound of the motor or the movement of water spraying outward from the bow to stern as the boat forced its way through the water. But now the only sounds she could hear were soft waves lightly splashing against the side of the boat, and a gull overhead... screeching for a chance to grab an impending scrap taken from a trap.

The anticipation of the moment was as if a theater curtain were about to rise and introduce a play to an anxious audience waiting for what was to follow. Alexandra and Taso were now alone in this vast, silent, natural theater, and the next act was about to be set into motion.

Taso had now turned his attention to Alexandra, and spoke lovingly to her, saying, "Before we begin, I have a special gift for you so that this day will become a lasting memory for us." Then, he moved toward the ornately trimmed box that held the linen napkin that had spoken of the love between his father and mother. He opened the chest and reached below the napkin to retrieve a small black velvet box. He approached Alexandra with the box, and looking deeply into her eyes, he handed it to her and said… "This is for you."

Alexandra's surprised expression revealed a soft blush as Taso placed the box into her hands. She stood there for a moment, not knowing what to say or do, but Taso again spoke, "Go ahead and open it."

With an excited tremble in her hands, Alexandra carefully opened the black velvet box. When opened, it contained a small gold, heart-shaped locket attached to a thin gold chain. Alexandra gasped in excitement, and squealed out, "Oh my… it's beautiful!" Taso was relieved to hear the delight in her voice as Alexandra removed the locket from the box and stared lovingly at it.

"Open it Alex," Taso instructed… and Alexandra slowly spread the two-sided heart apart to reveal the insides of the locket.

Within the right side heart was a small photo of Taso smiling, wearing his sailor's uniform, and his sailor's hat slightly tilted over his forehead. His features were strong and handsome, and the expression on his face was one of trust and confidence.

Alexandra continued to stare lovingly at the image and then replied… "I love it, and now I can have you with me all the time." Then, she shifted her eyes to the left side of the locket where a molded silver image of an angel holding a sword pointed toward a serpent that was being forced to the ground in submission.

Alexandra knew the image well, as she proclaimed, "It's Michael, the Archangel!" Taso spoke again, "Yes, and he'll protect you like he has protected me and my family for generations."

Tears filled Alexandra's eyes as she moved toward Taso, placing her arms around him and burying her head once again into his chest, pausing to reflect on the gift of love. Then she whispered to him, "I love you so much, and this locket is so beautiful… thank you." Taso whispered back, "I love you too, and between Michael and I, you'll have love and protection always close to your heart."

They held each other for a long time, as the little boat bobbed freely in the vastness of the sea. God had placed the two together and sealed their love with the protection of His most trusted servant, Michael the angel. The day surely would be one that remained in their own hearts forever, as they journeyed toward the dream when they would exchange vows and create a new covenant with their Master.

"Well," Taso said, "now it's time to see what gifts we have below the water." While Taso and Alexandra may have been seemingly lost in the loving exchange of words and the locket, the boat was not wandering aimlessly in the water. Taso actually had guided the boat so that it was alongside of one of his buoy's that displayed the colors of the Greek flag. His white buoy with blue stripes and a white cross on its side bobbed gently alongside the boat, only a few feet from its rail.

"This is the first trap on the trap line," Taso said with a tone of pride in his voice. "There are other lines farther out along this ledge, but this line is about eight fathoms below the boat. I've been very lucky with my catch here, even though the water is deep and near the rocky drop-off of the ledge. I want to show you what it's like to be a lobsterman, and you can help me bring up a trap."

Taso had barely finished his words when Alexandra leaped from the engine compartment where she had been sitting, and then moved toward him, removing her jacket and beginning to roll up the sleeves of her sweatshirt. "Hold on now," Taso said with a grin. "You must first put on this pair of oilskins to keep you dry," as he reached inside the pilothouse to snag a pair of baggy, shiny yellow pants and handed them to her, saying, "Slip them on over your dungarees, and make sure that they're comfortable."

Alexandra curiously examined the strange yellow pants, but then awkwardly attempted to step into them... almost losing her balance and falling. Taso reached for her arm to steady her movements. When she had finally gotten into the oilskins, she looked up at Taso, and with a smile on her face; she planted her fists on her hips saying, "Okay Captain, how do I look?"

It was all Taso could do to hold back his laughter, for the contrasting beauty of Alexandra wearing her gold locket and the baggy well-worn oilskins was an image that he would never forget.

He smiled back at her and said, "You look like a fisherman, how do you feel in them?"

"Awkward!" She exclaimed... they don't bend very much, how do you move along the boat all day in these?" Taso was not aware of how stiff the oilskins actually were, for he was strong and never noticed the resistance.

"You'll get used to them," Taso assured her. Alexandra replied with a determined voice, "I can do anything, watch me," as she moved to the rail where she anticipated the adventure would begin. Taso chuckled as he put on his own oilskins, and readied himself to begin hauling up a trap.

"Okay, let's see what we've caught," Taso said as he reached for the gaff used to snag the buoy. "First we've got to get the buoy into the boat. The trap is somewhere below it tied to this warp... I mean rope." Taso was aware of the strange language used for gear on a boat, and wanted Alexandra to be comfortable with the explanation. Then again, reaching into the pilothouse he started the boat's motor and lifted a switch, which then started a loud mechanical pulley. "We call this a pot hauler... it's a hydraulic pulley that'll help us lift the heavy traps out of the water, and into the boat.

"Years ago we had to pull the traps up by hand, and by the end of the day I could hardly move my arms. Sometimes a trap gets dragged along the bottom of the ocean, and can snag there when it collects a lot of sand and debris, making it too heavy to lift. This makes bringing the traps to the surface much easier, and I can handle more traps in a day than I did before having it."

The pulley began spinning very fast as Alexandra instinctively stepped back away from it. "Very good!" Taso replied, "This equipment can be very dangerous and must be respected. A lot of injuries have occurred to fishermen who got a rope or something snagged in the pulley. You remember when four or five years ago Shawn Foster hurt his arm and shoulder really bad when his sleeve got caught in the warp being pulled through the pulley. Fortunately, I was in my boat, fishing close-by, when I heard his voice after he got tangled in that warp. Luckily, I got there just in time to save his arm from being torn off. Shawn's arm and shoulders were seriously damaged, and after that incident he couldn't use his arms very well to haul traps or fish. Anyway, always be aware of the pot hauler pulley and where the warps... I mean ropes are lying on the deck."

Alexandra's eyes were opened wide as she held on to every word Taso was saying. She knew Shawn well, and how the injury had affected her friend's life, and she was not about to let that happen to her.

Taso then reached for the buoy, and grabbed the warp, placing it carefully onto the spinning pulley, explaining, "The pulley will lift the trap out of the water until the toggle comes up... Oh, the toggle is a small float that keeps the warp... I mean rope." At this, Alexandra laughed and said, "Don't worry, I know what a warp is now so call it a warp. And a toggle is a float, let's keep calling it a toggle... in no time I'll learn all the language. Now, what were you going to say about the toggle?" Taso was surprised and impressed that Alexandra was latching onto his every word, and seemed interested in what was going on within the boat.

"Well," Taso said with a smile on his face, "as I was saying, the toggle is an underwater float that keeps the line positioned just above the trap, keeping it from snagging onto seaweed or rocks. Without it, I could lose a trap. Anyway, when the toggle comes up out of the water, it jams into the davit on the pot hauler pulley and stops the trap at just the right position for me to grab onto it. Then I'll pull it over the rail to see what we've caught."

At that very moment, a small cork-like float appeared on the warp just coming over the rail and rapidly moving toward the pulley. Alexandra kept her eyes on the moving toggle, almost expecting it to be eaten up by davit in front of the spinning pulley. But just as Taso said would happen, the toggle jammed into the davit and it stopped. She looked up at Taso who was watching her intense concentration on what was going on in the boat.

After the heavy trap appeared as expected, Taso effortlessly lifted it onto the rail. The box-like trap looked like a small cage with horizontal wood slats. From between the slats, water spewed outward onto the deck and over the rail. Between the open spaces in the slats Alexandra could see the insides, and what appeared to be an indistinguishable mass of seaweed, sand and moving creatures frantically grabbing at the air with their pincher-like claws.

Taso directed his attention to the trap and instinctively reached for an almost hidden door that he opened to allow him to explore the treasures within. "Yes," he said as he reached in to grab seaweed, which he threw back into the water. "We have a good pull here, and the buyers will also like what we have."

Taso then began taking lobsters out of the trap and measuring them with a tool that distinguished "keepers" from those too small or too large to keep. He placed the keepers into a basket on the deck and some clams in a box alongside the basket.

After a short time, the trap was cleared, and Taso exclaimed, "Let's see... we have four keepers, about six clams and two urchins. I'll keep everything but the urchins." Then, without any concern for what he was about to do, he tossed the urchins into the water.

What followed surprised Alexandra, as she watched the urchin's fall toward the water? Almost as if the sky had released a missile toward the boat, a hungry gull swooped down toward the water and snatched one of the urchins as it hit the water's surface. Taso saw what had just happened, and said in a somewhat apologetic way, "Nature has a way of accounting for all its creatures... and some may lose their life, while others seem to benefit from it. I'll never understand it, but God must know what's best for all of us."

Alexandra was surprised at how effortlessly the gull snatched the urchin, and was now flying away to some unknown place where it would partake in its newly obtained meal.

Tears entered her eyes, as her mood changed rapidly from one of carefree happiness to sadness, all because a simple life form like an urchin had lost its life. Normally, Taso would not have thought much about what had happened because it was a common occurrence on a lobster boat, but now he saw how Alexandra was touched by the seemingly simple loss of an urchin's life.

Taso was seeing in Alexandra a deep profound love for life, no matter how simple the creature was. Within himself, he too began to reflect on the meaning of life.

Taso's mood began to change just like Alexandra's, and leaving the trap on the rail he approached her in a comforting manner, gently placing his hands in hers. Then, he spoke, "You're so special, and God sees your love for all creatures. He's placed us here because so many people cannot, or don't understand how we're to mingle our lives together in harmony with all creatures. I don't understand it myself, but I trust that if we respect all of God's creatures, man or animal, we're doing what's best, and God will smile on us."

At these words, Alexandra replied, "It's not so much that the urchin will die, but I was thinking about how important life is, and how so unexpectedly it can change. Nature and the sea can be so unpredictable, and you're out in it every day. You're on this boat, alone, in the vastness of the sea... with spinning wheels and heavy traps and ropes... I mean warps." Taso and Alexandra both smiled as she self-corrected her newly learned language.

She continued, "I'll always worry about you, and I know that God sees you as a special person too, and will protect you from harm. I can see why your mother always worried about your father, and why the napkin was so important. I'll always worry about you, but after all, we do have Michael the angel to look over us, and he'll always be at our side," as she placed her hand over the locket. It was now Alexandra who was comforting Taso, and their bonding spirits echoed their mutual respect for all of God's creatures.

Taso was becoming aware of how Alexandra was teaching him about things that he rarely thought of before, and was feeling comfort in her presence.

"Well," Taso said, "let's thank God today for the blessings that He's given us," then he turned toward the basket holding the keepers, and picked it up, walked to the rail… and tossed the lobsters back into the water. As the lobsters splashed into the water Taso spoke to them, much as one would say good bye to a good friend parting company, "Farewell my little friends, you'll live to see another day, and not to worry, we'll pray for your friend the sea urchin."

Alexandra was stunned at what Taso had done and exclaimed, "You can't do that, you're a fisherman and this is your livelihood." Taso answered, "Yes it is, but today I'll release the lobsters in thanks for you being here with me and helping me understand the depth of love and the profound meaning of life. Another day, I'll catch lobsters, but today, we'll celebrate life and the blessings that God has given us."

While Taso knew that, as a fisherman, he could take from the sea what would be allowed for life and sustenance, he would never hurt a creature, or abuse the benevolence that God bestowed upon him. Alexandra looked on in loving amazement, for she was seeing the true spirit of the man she would marry, and it touched the depth of her soul.

Chapter Eight

Taso and Alexandra spent the next hour or so sitting close to one another, as if in silent prayer, meditating on all that was said and happened. Taso had been at this spot many times before, always being drawn to its beauty. Now they were together, sharing a piece of God's creation.

What drew him to this spot was always a mystery, but one that left him with a feeling of peace. No one could dispute the beauty of this special place, as they looked toward the shore where they could see the land rising from the water, and a line of tall white pines on the hills a short distance away. Directly in front of them was a granite cliff that rose sharply upward, ending in a slender pointed statue-like shape, resembling two hands folded in prayer.

"Do you see that, Alex," as he pointed to the statue-like hands... "Those are hands praying for all the fishermen in the Cove." Alexandra stared toward the cliff and gasped in excitement, saying, "Oh yes, they are hands, and they're folded in prayer, you could never see them from the land." Taso responded, "Yes, those hands remind us that the sea will provide what we need, but only if we trust in Him."

For a long time, the couple continued to marvel at the beauty of this spot, hands locked together with shoulders touching, and their faces pointed toward this natural stage.

Taso thought back to his father's description of Eden. He could only wonder if this place were not the same one as legend had proclaimed, where nature itself was displaying its own story of time.

Above the boat, the sun had moved from low in the sky to almost directly above them, warming their bodies as they stared at the land in front of them. Taso broke the silence, saying, "Being here with you at this place has made it special for us, and we'll come back often to remind us of who we are. The sounds of the ocean and the feel of the breeze across my face has been soothing and dulled my awareness of what time it is."

Alexandra straightened up from her laid back position against Taso' body and said, "What do you mean, what time is it?"

Taso laughed and replied, "My stomach is telling me that it's time to see what's in that basket you brought."

With all that was going on in the boat, Alexandra had almost forgotten about the basket, and teased Taso by saying, "You've not done much work this morning so how can you be hungry?" Taso laughed back, "I'm always hungry, and you'll have to keep me fed, and that may prove to be your biggest challenge after we're married."

"Okay my Captain" she replied, "I better feed you before you're too weak to hold me in your strong arms." Both Taso and Alexandra rose from their comfortable spot on the warm engine compartment and began to move about in the boat.

Taso noticed that the open lobster trap was still sitting on the rail, and had not been baited and returned to its resting place below the boat. "I better bait this trap and put it back before we stop for lunch. You can help me with it so that you've experienced the whole cycle of Lobstering, because some day you might want to become my Sternman helper, and actually get paid for doing this." Then, looking over to a bucket containing pieces of ripe fish heads, used for bait, he reached in and grabbed a bait sack and placed it in the trap. "Now we're ready to put it back, but be careful when the warp rushes over the rail as I push it over the side, the trap will drop very fast and pull the warp along with it."

Alexandra quickly moved next to Taso and begged, "Let me do it, I've only watched you work, and it's about time that I do something for my pay."

"Okay my love... then you must try it," Taso answered, as he stepped back to watch Alexandra return the trap into the water.

Alexandra carefully looked the trap over to see how she would approach it to toss it overboard.

The trap was large and heavy, with splinter-like edges that could cut into her soft skin... and besides; this would be a challenge of her strength and agility. She didn't want Taso to think that she couldn't do such a simple thing as toss a trap into the water. So, with arms opened wide to grasp as much of the trap as possible, she pressed her body forward, and placed her chin on the top of the trap to get balance. Then she began to lift the trap to push it over the rail. The Captain looked on with pride as he watched the determined Alexandra show him that she could be a worthy helper, and hold her own.

Normally, the Captain was well tuned to the natural rhythms of the sea, but somehow he lost his awareness of the surroundings as he fixed his total attention on Alexandra attempting to put the trap back into the water. He failed to notice that the warm temperature that they were enjoying all morning had abruptly turned bitter cold, even though the skies were clear blue with no wind.

He also didn't notice that the water below the boat had changed color from a deep blue to a dark ink-black, almost iridescent color. The boat was beginning to roll back and forth as if in the wake of another boat... but no other boat was in the area. Uncharacteristically, all of the changes occurred in only a brief moment, as the boat pitched from side-to-side, even though waves were not present.

Standing became difficult and Taso finally was aware of the suddenness of the changes. He reached toward Alexandra to help stabilize her movements while she struggled with the trap, but he wasn't quick enough.

Then, the unthinkable happened so quickly that neither Taso nor Alexandra could react to avoid it. The boat suddenly jerked upward while Alexandra was struggling with the heavy trap, and she lost her balance as the trap went over the rail, almost dragging her with it.

Without warning, Alexandra's gold locket chain snagged on the edge of the trap and was torn from her neck as it followed the trap into the water, flashing its heart shaped form as it momentarily paused on the surface, as if mocking what had happened.

Not only were the locket and trap dragged overboard, but also Alexandra was being dragged toward the water. Under her breath she gasped in shock, "Oh no!" at what had just happened, eyes fixed on the spot where she saw the locket being swallowed by the cold slushy ink-black waters below.

Taso instinctively grabbed the gaff and plunged it toward the dark waters to try to snag the trap and locket before they disappeared, but his aim was thwarted by the rocking boat, and the gaff came out empty.

The boat continued to rock side-to-side, as Alexandra was sent backward onto the wet slippery deck, where her head hit the engine compartment. In a daze, she tried to get back on her feet, only to be thrust forward onto the deck by the rolling motion of the boat. Taso could barely maintain his own footing, even though he had spent decades standing on the deck of many boat's in violent seas.

With all his strength, Taso struggled over to Alexandra as she grabbed for his hands. Lifting her to her feet, he pulled her close to him along the rail, asking, "Are you okay?"

With sadness in her eyes and a trembling voice she responded, "Yes, I'm okay... but the locket... it's gone!" Then she stared over the rail where they had watched as the trap and locket had disappeared into the black water below.

Realization had begun to set in for what had just happened and Alexandra held onto Taso, repeating over and over, "Oh... I'm so sorry... how clumsy I am... how clumsy I am." Taso felt Alexandra's pain, and pulled her closer to him to protect her from the protesting angry sea.

Alexandra's weakened body sunk into Taso's as her trembling body shook both of them. She tearfully kept pleading for Taso's forgiveness, "Oh Taso, I'm so sorry. The locket was so beautiful and I lost it, I'm so sorry... I'm so clumsy."

The locket was of no concern at this time, for Alexandra's safety was dominating the Captain's' actions as he held her tightly, bracing his body against the pilothouse so that the boat's movements would not harm them. All the while, he kept trying to ease her concern for the lost locket, holding her in a child-like embrace, offering her words of assurance, "Don't worry Alex, it's okay, everything's okay," He kept holding on tightly as the strange unexplained mood of the sea intensified its relentless spell over the boat.

As the boat continued to rock back and forth, the rail's edge moved closer and closer to the water line with each thrust, water spilling onto the deck and threatening to sink the boat. Taso held on to Alexandra even tighter, thinking about what he would do if the boat sunk. Fear entered his own brain as he realized that they weren't wearing life jackets, and a plunge into these cold waters could be fatal for the both of them.

The boat continued to rock back and forth, and when it finally pitched deeply toward the starboard side, water engulfed the couple, and the boat took on far too much water to stay afloat. As the cold water poured off their bodies, they gasped with shock, choking and spitting out the frigid water as they tried to catch their breaths.

The Captain watched with concern as the *Eagles Wing's* rolled back toward the Port side where even more water came in, completely submerging the deck. They would not be able to hold on much longer as they braced for what might be the last pitch of the boat before it went under.

Then, on the last roll before the boat would be completely swamped by water, the clapper on the Ship's bell struck the bell's side, sending its resonating sound pealing outward. The boat rolled back the other way, and once again the bell sent its piercing sound across the water.

Then, as if the sound of the bell was speaking to the vicious sea, its mood instantly responded, and with one last roll, the *Eagles Wing's* lifted upward off the water as if unseen hands were cradling the boat for protection. Water that had filled the deck began to reverse its direction, spilling back into the sea, as if it had been commanded to do so.

The boat's rolling motion lessened, and then finally stopped as the boat once again settled on the calming waters. The chill in the air had subsided and was replaced by the warm rays of the sun. The black iridescent water turned a pale blue-green color as the seas continued to settle down. The frightened couple could feel the warm rays of the sun begin to dry their wet bodies, and remarkably, in only a few moments their soaked clothes were almost completely dry.

Taso and Alexandra continued to hold on to each other as confusion clouded their minds as they struggled to try to understand what had just happened.

Somewhere deep in Taso's dream-like thoughts, he was visualizing bleak images of a treacherous sea and a boat with two people on it, a man and a small child. He couldn't recognize the people or the place, but for now, he would have to forego his dream for a later time.

Once again he turned his attention back to Alexandra, whose drained body stood frozen within his arms. A few moments passed, and the fear that had gripped them was replaced by calm as the boat bobbed carelessly on the water, as if nothing had happened. The only sound that remained was the screeching of a gull overhead, awaiting a morsel of food that might be tossed overboard.

Taso slowly released his grip on Alexandra, and instinctively grabbed the warp that held the trap. Once again he placed the line over the pot hauler to draw the trap back up. Perhaps the locket had not come free from the trap as it slipped into the water, and it would emerge safely, tangled within the sharp edges of the trap that had snagged the locket from Alexandra's neck. Seconds later the trap emerged as it followed the warp toward the rail. Taso grabbed the trap as it reached the surface, and gently placed it once again on the rail. In silence, they both examined the trap, hoping for a miracle. Carefully Taso opened the trap door and stared inside. His heart sank as nothing but a few pieces of seaweed lay inside. This day there would be no miracle... for the trap was as empty as their spirits at what had happened.

The ravages that the sea had placed upon them, and the realization of losing the locket overcame Alexandra. Feelings of sadness and guilt flooded her thoughts, weakening her to the point that if she were to let go of Taso, she might not be able to stand. Taso continued to hold on to Alexandra, and knew that she needed him more than ever before. Tears continued down Alexandra's face as she wept uncontrollably in her Captain's arms.

Finally, Taso broke the silence, saying, "Alex, don't worry about the locket, we're safe, and we've got each other, and that's all that matters. The locket was only a piece of metal, and only a symbol of our love, and it can be replaced. Symbols are one thing, but our love for one another is more powerful than anything we'll ever encounter."

Then for a moment, Taso's mind flashed thoughts of how the unexplained forces that overcame the boat were the reason for the loss of the locket, and not Alexandra's carelessness. He pondered to himself, perhaps a nearby whale trying to surface caused the boat to roll, or maybe a giant squid, like Crock once described, caused the water to turn the dark ink-black color? He thought of how the sea was home to many creatures, some very large and silent in their movements, and perhaps that could explain what happened. He recalled all the stories told by seamen in the pubs back in the Cove, but dismissed them because they were most likely only embellished stories. But what about the rapid cold temperature that overcame the boat, the sky was clear blue and the sun was shining all the time? The Captain puzzled over the situation, for he had never experienced so many unexplained things before.

He thought for a moment about the story his father told him as a child, and how Michael the angel would always be on the boat to protect it. Surely, someone or something had intervened to bring them to safety moments after the bell pealed out its sound.

Then he continued to comfort Alexandra, "We have each other, and no object or symbol can ever take its place... and for the Archangel, his image may be at the bottom of the sea, but he must have been with us when the boat began to rock and we weren't harmed. I don't know what just happened, but the sea can act strange at times, and I guess that's what happened, and the bell... I just don't know." Again he quizzed his knowledge and experience for an explanation, but none was there.

"It wasn't you Alex, who did anything wrong, it just happened and you're okay and that's all that matters. We'll be married soon and we'll be tested many times when unexpected things enter into our lives. But we'll endure them because we don't have to endure them alone, we have each other to provide the strength... and maybe, just maybe, the angel will be with us when we need him most."

Alexandra felt comfort in Taso' words, as she paused to reflect on them. Only a few moments ago she was overcome with terror as the seas threatened their lives, but now she found peace in the arms of the Captain. Not only did he physically protect her on the boat, but also, he was responding to her emotional needs in a way that most men could never do. She felt safe and protected in Taso' arms, as a feeling of calm began to replace the grief over losing the locket and the fear she had while being thrown around the boat.

Alexandra looked up into her Captain's eyes, and spoke of the depth of their love, saying, "I do love you more than anything on earth, and I know that life isn't always perfect. I was so frightened while the boat was rocking and water was coming in. I'm not sure that I could have survived being out here alone.

The thought of how you're out on the ocean day-after-day, and things like this can come up so suddenly and threaten to harm you. Your mother must have worried so much about your father when he was on the boat, no wonder each day she waited for his safe return. I can't say that I won't worry about you when you're out here fishing... because I will. And I know that you're a wise fisherman and you know how to do the right things when trouble approaches, but what about the unexpected things that can harm you without warning? Will the angel always be here to protect us? And yes, the locket was only a symbol of our love. But it wasn't so much that the locket was a beautiful symbol, it was that it made me feel so special... close and safe with both you and the angel as my protectors. And the way you gave it to me on this boat, at this special place... I'll never forget what it means. You're right, our love is greater than what any object can reveal about us, and I'll always feel safe when you're with me. I trust in you and the angel for protection, we're truly blessed to have one another."

No more needed to be said, for their love had been tested by disharmony in the sea, and they survived the test. Their souls were united in a common bond of love, blessed by the promise of peace and protection by an unseen angel. This would be the foundation of their marriage, and the conquering element for anything that would come to test their love for one another.

The memory of what had happened that morning on the boat would not be forgotten, for they would often recall the strength and profound intimacy that was tested, and the realization that they were vulnerable to life's most challenging elements. Now, the Captain and Alexandra needed to distance their thoughts from what had happened that morning, and enjoy the little time they had before going back to the cove.

Alexandra, breaking the tension, teasingly spoke first, "Now my Captain, what'll we do if we're not going to catch lobsters today?" Taso was quick to reply as he once again looked toward the almost forgotten linen covered basket sitting on the deck inside the pilothouse, expecting it to be totally destroyed by the water that had come into the boat.

Remarkably, the basket was dry and strangely had not been affected by the drenching that both Alexandra and the Captain had experienced. The Captain just shook his head, not wanting to try to figure out another mystery. "Okay, we'll finally see what you've brought in that basket, and feed my starving body."

While hunger was the last thing that they needed to satisfy, they both felt it was necessary to do something to change the scene, and what better would there be than to share a good meal. Alexandra moved to the basket and lifted it up to the engine compartment, slowly removing the linen cover to reveal its contents. Taso leaned forward in anticipation as Alexandra quickly put her arm between the basket and Taso. "Be patient my love, I have to do some preparation before we eat, is there something that you can do elsewhere on the boat while I do this?"

In a somewhat playful manner, Taso backed up a few steps and forced a makeshift frown on his face, pouting like a disappointed child, saying, "Well, if I have to." Then he walked into the pilothouse to tend to some spare traps needing repair.

Alexandra proceeded to set the makeshift table for their meal. She placed the fresh linen tablecloth on the engine compartment, smoothing out any wrinkles as she went. Then came out the matching white linen napkins and a candle for the center of the table. Bone china plates and silver place settings followed, and a single rose was laid across each setting. She then reached deeper within the basket and began to remove the food, placing the items in deliberate fashion, as if they could only be placed in pre-assigned spots. The food had been prepared with love, and total attention to perfection, lacking nothing, and spread out completely across the festive makeshift table.

Alexandra loved to cook and had created this special meal using recipes that had been in her family for centuries and included many traditional Greek specialties. There was fresh feta cheese placed alongside of a loaf of crusty bread. A shallow bowl of kefthetes (small meatballs made with tomato, garlic and herbs) occupied the center of the banquet. Next to the kefthetes was spanakopita (a traditional spinach and feta cheese pie). Traditional dolmades (stuffed grape leaves) were placed among the other main courses, and released an aroma that seemed to knit everything together. A cucumber, tomato and feta cheese salad laced with fresh basil filled out the vegetable course, leaving only dessert and wine to complete the meal.

The finishing touches were not forgotten, and hidden beneath a linen napkin was a plate of baklava (filo pastry baked to a glossy golden color, and layered with nuts and honey). Sitting in front of the banquet, in-between two tall wine glasses, was a bottle of Retsina wine (a special vintage indigenous to Greece since ancient times, and used only for special celebrations).

The banquet was ready, as Alexandra peered across the table one last time to be sure that nothing was missing... and her smile was proof that indeed, nothing was missing. She thought silently to herself... certainly Taso would enjoy the meal, and besides, she would now have a chance to find out what foods he really liked so that as his wife she would always be ready to please him.

Then, she called to Taso. "My Captain, the banquet awaits your presence!" Taso turned from within the pilothouse at the sound of Alexandra's voice, and approached her with a look of anticipation on his face.

Alexandra spoke again before Taso reached the table, "Now don't forget to wash your hands." Taso smiled, as he recalled his mother's same instructions as a child. But, he was already prepared for the request, as evidenced by the small towel he held in his hands, as he was wiping them clean.

His eyes immediately were drawn to the table and his face lit up like a child gazing on a Christmas tree on Christmas morning. Taso continued to stare at the elegant table and shook his head in disbelief, saying, "Oh my God, that's amazing... and look, candles and china and linens, the food and everything. You must have worked all day and night to prepare this."

Alexandra smiled and said, "For you I would spend an eternity to make you feel happy, and besides, you are my Captain and I am your mate... well, I will be your mate very soon, and I'll be responsible for your wellbeing. I hope that there will be room in the box for one of these napkins."

Together they looked toward the ornately trimmed box that held within it the napkin that bridged the love of Taso's parents. Taso responded with words that would start a new tradition, "Yes Alex, I will place your napkin next to my mother's, and I promise to always bring it back home safely to you. Our dreams will soon become a reality when we are married, and I'll not be going home to an empty house, but to our house where you and I will share our love in each other's arms."

Alexandra reached for the bottle of Retsina wine and filled the glasses, and then handed one to Taso, awaiting his toast. He looked into her eyes, lifted the glass high toward his lover, and said, "Today we share the blessings that God has given us. May our hearts become one, and our bodies be nourished by the food you have prepared. And with God's blessing, we will always know the power of our love."

The glasses sought each other as their rims touched, sending a whispering "cling," sound pealing across the water... and the precious red liquid touched their lips in affirmation of the blessing.

The loving couple then embraced, sharing their love, knowing that they could endure anything that tried to threaten it.

Chapter Nine

The couple's dreams would be realized a year later when many of their friends in Black Point Cove would celebrate their marriage together in Saint Finbarr's Church overlooking the sea.

Shawn Foster had become Taso's best friend and had accepted the honor of being the Best Man for the couple's wedding. And Megan, being the closest friend to Alexandra would naturally become her Matron of Honor for the ceremony.

The morning of their wedding finally arrived, as Taso anxiously waited in front of the church sanctuary, as if in a trance, staring toward the back in anticipation of his bride.

Within the church, friends filled the pews, all ready to witness the marriage of Alexandra to the fisherman. The newly ordained Father Charles Benning would preside over the ceremony, and was standing in the center of the church, in front of the alter. In his hands he held an open book that contained the words and vows that would be proclaimed during the ceremony. This was the Priest's first wedding ceremony, and he nervously anticipated what was about to unfold.

Father Benning was anxiously chattering on and on to Taso about almost anything to pass the time before the ceremony would begin. "How nice it would be if the steeple on the Church had a bell in it, to ring after the ceremony," he spoke to Taso, but Taso was not concentrating on what the Reverend Father Benning was saying because of the tense expectation of his bride's appearance.

While Taso had endured the stresses of war, and many difficult moments at sea, always finding strength in the challenge, his body was feeling weak and frail as he awaited his bride.

The guests sat motionless, with their heads turned toward the back of the church, waiting for the signal that would announce the beginning of the ceremony. Then, breaking the tension of the moment, the church organ interrupted the silence, as Brautchor's classical wedding march began its introduction of what was to come.

With all eyes riveted to the back of the church, Megan, appeared from around the corner, wearing a simple, soft pink cotton dress, and holding a bouquet of white daises mixed with purple Lupines... the native flower of Maine. When Megan had reached about halfway down the aisle, almost magically, the graceful figure of Alexandra suddenly appeared in the back of the church.

Alexandra's beauty was stunning, as she turned toward the front of the church to begin her procession down the aisle. She wore a softly flowing pearl-white lace wedding dress that loosely draped over the subtle curves of her slim frame. The dress's glimmering sheen was accented with subtle lace highlights, not too bold as to take away from Alexandra's natural beauty, but to compliment her with its elegant simplicity.

A braided ring bouquet circled her head, and was adorned with fragrant white and pink sea roses, delicately placed within baby's breath trim. In her hands she held a simple but elegant bouquet of white sea roses, interlaced with English ivy and baby's breath. A flowing lace veil with edges trimmed with mother-of-pearl beads emerged from the ringed crown of sea roses and flowed downward over her shoulders and past her waist.

Taso couldn't help but feel a sudden rush of exhilaration as her slow steps silently revealed the glowing figure of his bride's approach.

Alexandra's dark eyes were fixed low and in front of her as she slowly glided along the aisle, as if she were floating on air. Candle stands placed every few feet apart along the aisle flickered their warm dancing images off of Alexandra's shimmering gown, as she moved closer and closer toward her lover. Her face held the smile that had captivated so many, but had now captured the man awaiting her arrival only a few steps away.

When Megan finally reached the front of the Alter, she turned and stepped toward Shawn, where she then stood at his side. Taso' eyes were transfixed on Alexandra, seeing her in a way that only true lovers could understand. The feeling of anticipation that had made him tense only moments before was replaced by confidence and excitement as Alexandra moved closer to him.

Taso could see her radiant face through the veil, as her hands met his, reminiscent of the day when they first touched in the gathering hall just a few steps away from this sacred spot. Today would be different, as their hands would now meet to receive golden rings placed on their fingers as symbols of eternal love.

The ceremony that followed was dignified and solemn, as the couple's testimony to their undying love were spoken in the presence of God and witnessed by their closest friends.

Father Benning began the ceremony by introducing the couple and then asking them to confirm their intentions for matrimony; "Anastasios and Alexandra, have you come freely to give yourselves to one another, and will you honor each other as man and wife for the rest of your lives?"

"We do!" was their shared reply as they joyfully looked into each other's eyes.

"Will you accept children lovingly from God, and bring them up according to the law of Christ and His church?"

"Yes, we will!" they replied in unison, as their moist eyes continued to stare unbroken into one another's.

Father Benning proceeded on with holy petitions asking God to bestow his blessings on the couple, as the proclaiming of their vows was about to begin. "Since it is your intention to enter into holy marriage, join your right hands, and declare your consent to God and his Church"

Taso and Alex joined hands as the Priest led the vows by instructing Taso to declare them to Alexandra; "I Anastasios Christos Pappas, take you Alexandra, to be my lawful wife. I promise to be true to you in good times and in bad, in sickness and in health. I will love you and honor you all the days of my life."

Then Father Benning looked toward Alexandra and instructed her to declare her vows to Taso... and as tears welled in her eyes she followed with the words; "I Alexandra Savallas, take you Anastasios to be my lawful husband. I promise to be true to you in good times and in bad, in sickness and in health. I will love you and honor you all the days of my life."

From within the crowd of friends gathered to witness the marriage, joyful sobs could be heard, as handkerchiefs wiped tears of happiness from their eyes.

After the vows were declared, simple gold rings were blessed by Father Benning, and then given to the couple to place upon one another's fingers as they spoke one after another; "Let this ring be a sign of my fidelity and love for you." For a moment, Alexandra struggled to slide Taso's ring over his broad finger, but eventually the ring found its place... over the hushed chuckles from the friends watching every movement in front of the alter.

At the conclusion of the vows and the exchange of the rings, the blessing hands of the Reverend Father Benning reached over the couple's heads as he proclaimed. "I now pronounce you man and wife. What God has joined together, nothing can separate."

The guests immediately stood up and cheered, applauding with zeal as Taso and Alexandra embraced one another and kissed to seal their vows.

What could not be heard over the applause in the Church was the resonating sound of a small Ship's bell on a colorful little fishing boat in the harbor. And while there was no one tugging on the bell's rope, the boat gently swayed from side to side in the water, making the bell clapper contact its sides, ringing it as if it were sealing their vows... "Ding-ding; Yes-yes" to what had taken place in the presence of God and man. The wedding ceremony had finally concluded, with affirmation from its witnesses, and the resounding sound of a bell that would sing out its approval. Following the wedding ceremony, all went back into the gathering hall where the couple had first met.

In a small village like Black Point Cove, there were very few events that were cause for celebration, but this wedding was one that was well overdue and the guests welcomed the change from their normal workday routines. Shawn and Megan led the party as they poured the traditional Restina wine, and honored the newlyweds. The guests were quick to join in, clicking glasses filled with the rich red wine, and toasting good fortune to the loving couple.

A feast of traditional Greek foods were presented to the guests, much like the foods prepared by Alex and presented to Taso on the *Eagles Wing's* during their first trip on the boat. But this time there was even more, as the rich smell of tender roasted lamb crusted with garlic and herbs was served as the main course. Accompanying the lamb were platters piled high with stuffed grape leaves and spinach and feta cheese pie. Kalamata olives and tiropita (buttered filo dough layered with various cheeses) accompanied the platters, as bowls of kefthetes followed close behind. The guests were then treated to sweet desserts of baklava and other pastries as an ending to the traditional meal that had graced their lips.

After the dinner, to go along with the wine, glasses of imported Ouzo were sipped while listening to lively music streaming from the Bouzouki, a traditional Greek guitar and violin accompaniment. Since dancing is an integral part of Greek lifestyle, it certainly was a part of the Pappas wedding celebration. While each Greek island has a special unique *Chorus* circle dance associated with it, the island of Ikaria (where Alexandra was born) had its own *Karhiotiko choros* dance. As the men joined in this circle dance, stepping to the beat of the music... their arms were interlocked as each step increased in rhythm, until the pace became faster and louder as it unfolded. Often, single dollar bills would be thrown into the air in admiration of the wedding couple and the enjoyment of the music.

Sometimes, too much Ouzo might influence the dancers, and individuals would occupy the center of the circle to do a solo version on their own.

Even Crock joined in the *Karhiotiko choros dance*, attempting to do a clogging type dance, even though he had a bad leg. Nonetheless, he shuffled and twisted to the sounds of the Bouzoukis and violin as the crowd laughed and surrounded him, clapping with their hands held high over their heads.

Crock's entertaining dance finally ended when he stumbled backward after attempting to jump high into to air and spin, but ended up in the hands of his fellow mates... just before he was about to crash to the floor. Everyone laughed while his friends lifted him up by his arms and legs, and put him on a chair where he would be safe.

Certainly the wedding was one that would not be forgotten for a long time, as the guests enjoyed the gracious hospitality of the Pappas's.

After many long hours of feasting, drinking and dancing, the festivities took its toll on the crowd, and one by one the celebrants began to say their goodbyes, many of them bracing... or embracing one another as they left the hall, arm in arm.

It wasn't until almost two in the morning that the last four people, Taso, Alexandra, Shawn and Megan realized that everyone had parted, and it was time for them to end the celebration. A final toast was made as wine filled glasses clinked for the last time, signaling that the party was over...

at least for this day. The couples truly enjoyed being with one another, their friendship often taking them into the wee hours of the morning as they talked and shared their lives with each other. This day was special, and they hesitated to part company, but after all, the bride and groom were anxious to be alone.

As the couples finally parted for the evening, Shawn and Megan went one way and the newlyweds went another. As Taso and Alexandra walked hand-in-hand down the elevated pathway along the shoreline, they were heading toward the Captain's house where they would begin their lives as the Pappas's.

Overhead, a full moon and twinkling stars reflected light over the land, making the sandy soil mixed with crushed seashells along the path sparkle, as if they were made of stardust. When the newlyweds reached the familiar stone bench where they had spent many anxious hours dreaming of their pending marriage, they paused to reflect on the moment.

Alexandra spoke in a tender and loving voice, "Taso, I'm the happiest woman alive, and we'll never have to leave one another again. I love you more than anything in this world, and I want to be the best wife that I can be to you." Taso held onto Alexandra and spoke back, "Alexandra, I too am blessed to have you as my wife, and yes, we won't have to part any longer. This special place has always made me happy, and now I can share it with you. I have a special gift for you, and hope that it'll make you happy."

Alexandra looked puzzlingly at Taso's words, responding, "What surprise, what do you mean?" "Well" he answered, "This place has meant so much to us... we've spent our most cherished times here, looking out at the ocean and dreaming of our life together. We've always had to part and wait for the next time that we could share the view together again, often in each other's arms. So, I bought this land overlooking our dream spot, and we'll build a home here together where we'll never have to part."

Alexandra squealed with excitement, "You didn't... you did...

Oh Taso, this is so special, how could I ever be any happier. What a beautiful gift for us. There is no place on earth that is more beautiful... and we'll actually live here?" Taso replied, "Yes my love, this is where we'll live and have children, and they'll play along the shore and learn to love what we love so much. You can watch from the window as the children play along the ocean, and as I pass by in my boat, I'll ring the bell, and you can wave back to me... and the children can wave also."

Alexandra was overcome with joy, as tears rolled off her cheeks, and fell onto the shimmering pathway that was now theirs. She responded with euphoria, "Children... what a beautiful thought, what'll we have, boy's or girls?" Maybe we'll have both... how many should we have, what will we call them?"

Taso smiled as he watched his excited Alex dream new dreams, knowing that he would be part of them all.

Like times past, they hesitated leaving this spot, but now the sun breaking the horizon in a silent explosion of bright yellow-orange and purple colors interrupted the hesitation.

In their hearts they knew that this was a sign that promised new life and eternal love. With arms tucked around each other's waist, they parted for the old home where they would share a bed in one another's embrace... and a deep sleep would fall upon them.

It was late morning when the drowsy couple was awakened by the sounds of gulls squawking their disagreement over a scrap of food snatched from a bait bucket left on a boat in the harbor. They rolled over to face one another as warm flesh and silent smiles consummated their love, for they would begin their first day as Mr. and Mrs. Anastasios Pappas.

Each morning thereafter, Alexandra would wake first to prepare breakfast for her Captain. She would make sure that a clean, neatly folded linen napkin would be placed alongside his plate, always to vanish with him as he left for the boat. She too would, as did Marianas for Demetrius, wait in anticipation for the return of her Captain and the soiled napkin that signaled their safe return home.

Often within the village, the newlywed couple would be seen strolling together, hand-in-hand, always taking time to pause and greet their friends. Their lively spirit seemed to be contagious as they met and talked with them. They cared for all of the people of the village, and in unassuming ways would tend to their needs, giving those in need fish or other seafood gathered on the boat. Taso would always take time to help other fishermen do repairs on their boat's or freely help Shawn at his shop, never asking for anything in return.

Alexandra would often visit the sick, feeding or bathing them, or just being there to listen to their concerns. She did this, not as part of her job as a nurse at the hospital, but because she truly cared for anyone who was in need. And with the same concern and care they had for others, they paid special attention to one another.

What would guide and lead their lives was love... love for one another and love for others. And like a tidal wave, the love and compassion that they had for each other, and for all they met, would echo throughout the village of Black Point Cove.

Chapter Ten

The spot where the newlyweds would build their home was one of magic, and for a hundred years had been the dwelling place for those seeking peace and solitude. The natural stone bench along the path welcomed strollers to pause long enough to clear their minds of obstacles and the imperfections of life. Practically overtaking the stone bench were thick, thorny vines of red, white and pink Sea Rose that crept close enough to impart their fragrance to the path dwellers. Even if you didn't take time to pause and sit on the bench, you would always take time to bend over close to the vines and sniff the intoxicating fragrance of roses.

This was a place where dreams were dreamed, and important thoughts were dwelt upon. When one sat on the smooth stone bench, they were drawn into a meditative state, as the sights, sounds and smells of nature replaced the distractions that often brought them to this place.

Lost in nature, time was slowed and peace would often follow. Looking out over the sea, a hundred feet or so down the smooth granite step-like slope, if you were lucky enough, you might see a dolphin appear and disappear as it glided along the surface.

An orchestra of seabirds sent sounds over the water that blended the squawks of gulls with the screeches of an Osprey swooping toward an unsuspecting fish to become a meal for its newly hatched chicks.

From this spot looking out toward the sea centuries ago, time had not changed what those first dwellers would have seen. But now, each morning a parade of lobster boat's streamed past, as the awaiting day drew the fishermen to their trap lines, promising gifts from the sea. Behind the bench, inward toward the village, life was changing rapidly as time seemed to move too fast for many.

The magic of the sea, which for a long time had kept many of the villagers close to it, was being replaced by the promise of other things that were drawing them inland, and away from it. However, Taso and Alexandra were different, and as much a part of the sea as the fish, birds, and water itself.

It was this spirit-of-the-sea that had convinced Taso to buy the land along the pathway where the smooth stone bench looked over the water. He and Alexandra had shared the spirit of the sea, and now they would build a home overlooking the spot where their souls were first united. They would create the design of the home together, and build it with the help of their friends on the Cove. The home would be positioned high upon the slope leading down to the water.

They would not disturb the pathway and stone bench, which still could be used by anyone in the Cove who sought the promise of peace and solitude.

Taso enlisted the help of his longtime friend Macias Crocket, to oversee the construction of the home. Although retired from shipbuilding, Crock was a master builder, and would see to it that every detail was correct and built to last. Skillfully, the master shipwright would fit each and every board close and tight, as if they would have to resist the pounding of a treacherous sea... although the sea's distance from the house would be of no concern.

The house would be built using as many natural materials as were present in the geography of Maine. Gray granite stone would be used for its foundation and fireplace... with dark gray inland slate finding its place on several floor areas and exterior walkways.

The larger than average, rectangular one story home would

have a "Widow's Watch" loft extending from the roof area, and looking out toward the open sea. The inside rooms would be open and spacious, casually spreading throughout the home. The only space not on the single first level home was the widow's watch loft, which was accessed by winding spiral steps leading up to the roof area. Entering through a narrow door opening onto the deck-like widow's watch, one would see a spectacular view of the Cove, as refreshing sea breezes swept across your body.

Broad, twelve paneled, double hung windows would occupy every room, each of which offered a panoramic view of the Atlantic Ocean.

The living room's large bay window offered the most spectacular interior view. Each day, if not obscured by fog, the early morning sunrise would show its first light, and illuminate the living room with its orange-yellow glow. Then, each morning, and again in the late afternoon, a parade of fishing boat's could be seen streaming past the window... putt-putting along in search of treasures to be given from the sea.

The open vaulted ceilings rose to a peak of almost sixteen feet in the main living room area and kitchen, and allowed warm summer air to rise upward, leaving cool comfortable spaces below.

Every feature built into the home would hint of the harmony of man and nature, and the promise of protection from anything that could harm them. Through the large bay window, the couple would often celebrate moments in a loving embrace, marveling at the beauty and mystery of the sea.

Good fortune preceded the building of the home when Crock learned of some wooden ship materials being stored in an abandoned warehouse in Bath, and were being thrown out by the owners. A quick call to the owners revealed that they were trying to empty the warehouse and were selling the lumber pieces as firewood. It was by luck that the Captain called the owners when he did, for he was allowed to purchase much of the needed lumber for his home, at scrap lumber prices.

When Taso and Crock visited the warehouse with Crock's flatbed truck, the sharp eye of the master shipwright and the Captain found pieces that could never be reproduced anywhere.

Long-leaf yellow pine planking taken from the forests around Jamestown, North Carolina, would have been used as deck planking for sleek sailing Ship's. But now these fine boards were abandoned as scrap, and would find its use as flooring within the new house. Hundreds of perfectly turned Locust wood trunnel pegs were chosen to join the post and beam framing together. For the railings on the winding staircase leading to the widow's watch loft, intricately turned mahogany balusters were found, and quickly put on Crock's truck.

Dozens of large, finely hewn Plantation White Oak beams were selected from a pile that had been neglected for decades, and would be used to tie the construction together. Crock commented as they struggled to lift the heavy beams onto the flatbed, "Dis is going to be tough ta cut or drills inta, but der strong and are gonna last ten lifetimes."

Wandering through the warehouse for additional materials, they spotted neatly piled small paneled oak doors that would be used on the kitchen cabinets. Rummaging further, a large stack of finely crafted full sized doors were uncovered, and would be used for most of the interior rooms. But a real treasure was discovered at the bottom of the pile of doors.

Below the dusty pile, were four intricately carved Mahogany doors that left Crock and the Captain in awe. After brushing away decades of accumulated dust on the doors, what was revealed was extraordinary.

Three of the four mahogany doors had six panels on them, each revealing intricately carved images of sea creatures or other animals. One door featured whales in various poses, while another featured dolphins breaching the water's surface in playful harmony with one another. The third door showed all sorts of smaller sea creatures, including sea horses, shellfish, crabs, snails and lobsters. The fourth door was almost four feet wide, and was the largest and heaviest... but also the most beautiful. On its four lower panels were striking images of Gulls, Puffins and other sea birds. But its most striking feature was a wide single top panel that occupied the full span of the door. Within the panel was a life-like sculpture of an open winged Osprey, perched on the edge of a ragged stick nest, and holding a small fish in its beak. Within the nest, overlooking the sea, was an Osprey chick... beak wide open and hungrily waiting for a meal. Not only was the door beautiful, but also the carvings within it looked so real, that one would expect the Osprey to take flight at any moment.

To add to the beauty of the doors, each came with cast bronze hinges and doorknobs with inserted whalebone scrimshaw carvings of different sailing Ship's. "Crock, look at these!" Taso exclaimed, knowing that Crock was also an accomplished scrimshaw carver. "These will work great for the bedrooms, and this one with the Osprey will make a welcome front door to the house. Crock gazed at the scrimshaw knobs and with a tone of awe in his voice he said, "Dis is amazing... da best I have ever laid me eyes on."

Both Crock and the Captain just kept smiling and shaking their heads in disbelief at the good fortune they had stumbled upon. For several more hours they scavenged through the warehouse, and found fine moldings and trim that would accent the home's nautical detail. By the time they finished loading the truck, they wouldn't be able to add a single toothpick to it.

Carefully they lashed the load to the truck and slowly drove away, both knowing that they had stumbled onto a master carpenter's dream... and purchased at fire wood prices.

All the way home Crock just kept saying, "Ya doesn't has any idea on how much material cost ya saved, and what special pieces ya now have. And it's good for ya that dey sold it to ya for scrap prices. Why, those doors alone would have cost the whole load." Crock was as excited as Taso was, and anxious to put his skills toward building the new home. When they finally got home, the pieces were unloaded and stacked into separate piles so that nothing would be hidden from the builder's eyes.

It didn't take long for the construction to begin, and soon, the foundation was in, followed by the post and beam frame construction. Taso and Crock guided the builders, and each special detail unfolded to create a home that was as much a part of the sea as would be a fine sailing ship.

The home was well built, using Crock's skills as a master boat builder, placing each beam and board together so that wind, rain nor snow could penetrate its walls. The finely hewn large oak beams dominated the open ceiling construction, and were assembled to resemble a long, upside-down ship's keel, where bulky support trusses ran perpendicular to the main keel-like beam at its peak. The long-leaf yellow pine planking filled in the spaces around the ceiling beams, and was varnished to a high gloss.

Large Locust wood trunnel pegs were hammered into holes drilled in the mortise and tenon joints, accenting the post and beam construction. Looking upward from any room, one would see what appeared to be the bottom-side of a Ship's belly supported by large vertical Douglas fir posts placed four feet apart along each span.

Within the open structure, interior walls separated the bedrooms, kitchen, bathroom and a large open living room. Between the vertical posts supporting the ceiling beams and trusses, were smooth plastered walls. The remainder of the yellow pine planking found its way as flooring throughout the home, and was treated with a high-gloss finish.

The glossy varnished post, beams and planking would reflect the dancing flames of a warm fire emerging from the gray granite fireplace, whose opening was shoulder high, and topped by a rugged oak beam that served as its mantle.

Alexandra had carefully chosen each stone for the fireplace, which would occupy the northeast face of the house. Using a wooden wheelbarrow with a steel wheel, the heavy stones were hauled up to the house, one load at a time. Then she would unload them in a neat pile and return back to the sea, where more stones would be gathered. Again and again Alexandra hauled load upon load up to the house.

When enough stones had been hauled up to the house, her blistered hands showed her determination for what she was doing... and not even a whisper of complaint ever left her lips. Alexandra was resolute and excited to see the house rise from its foundation. She felt a part of the conception of the house, and was now thoroughly taking part in its birth.

From outside of the house, the distinctive northern exposure revealed the massive stone fireplace wall, which offered a buffer for the many treacherous unannounced storms that could emerge from the northeast.

The outside frame walls were covered with hand-split cedar shake shingles that would weather naturally to a soft patina of gray with dark brown and black streaks melting downward as if it had rained colored ink upon its surface. The silver-gray slate roof would reflect the penetrating rays of the summer sun, keeping the inside cool... while during cold winter days the snow and ice would insulate the warm spaces below.

Three-plank, dark green shutters were placed alongside of the white painted window trim, giving the windows the appearance of wide-open eyes welcoming all of its visitors to its inner warmth and protection.

No matter what the weather offered, the home kept out the cold wet winds of winter and welcomed the refreshing sea breezes through its windows in summer.

Alex, Taso and Crock worked endless hours to finish the house in the shortest time possible, working far into the evening after many of the other workers went home. They had created a home that was filled with love, and would protect its inhabitants from anything that nature could throw its way. It only took three months to complete the home, and the anxious newlyweds were now filling its spaces with their own furnishings, many of which had their origins in Greece.

The house was special, and no other home in the Cove could

rival its uniqueness. The home and its stewards would become a part of the natural surroundings on the edge of the sea, where mountains gracefully approached the water. The home had been born with a rugged soul that was steeped in love and protection... and anyone who entered its walls was greeted by the winged image of an Osprey that welcomed you into the protection of its nest.

Chapter Eleven

During the war years when Taso had been assigned duty on the navel destroyer *USS Preble*, he often talked to his shipmates about how it was one of the finest old Ship's ever made because it was born of the skills and talents of the men of the Bath Iron Works. Taso loved the sea and his experience aboard the *Preble* gave him the opportunity to use his skills on his own boat.

Taso often pulled duty below deck in the engine room where he had become an accomplished master mechanic, servicing the drive engines of the *Preble*. His skills would not only come in handy later on his own fishing boat, but also when needed to help his friend Shawn at the repair shop.

When not working on engines or doing other repairs on the Preble, he spent endless hours polishing brass fittings to shine like gold. These same skills would follow him throughout life, as Taso knew that a simple tarnished fitting could decay quickly by the salt sea and might fail when it would be needed most.

Many times as a young boy aboard the *Eagles Wing's*, he was taught how to care for the "little things" that often became "big things" if not attended to properly. His seaman's skills, complimented by his mechanical skills would always come in handy when he needed them most.

Alex also influenced Taso in ways that would serve him well for all of his life. She was an example of patience and devotion, and persevered through difficult times without complaint.

She was often at Taso's side when helping build their house and would not hesitate to take on the most difficult tasks. It was not uncommon for Alex to emerge from chores with soot and smudges streaked across her delicate face, but always maintaining her smile and grace.

Her most precious gift to Taso was the way she taught him to be gentle and strong at the same time, a gift that many men could never master. Alexandra was kind, loving and slow to anger. She was a woman of strong faith and started each morning and ended each day with a prayer.

Taso would smile back at her when she finished a morning prayer, and she would say, "See, now God knows that I am awake and He will guide and protect me today."

While Taso didn't often show his spiritual side, he too knew that something deep inside always guided him when he was lost. He had been taught earlier by his father to always say a prayer before going out to sea, asking God to protect him and his family... so the assurances of Alexandra's prayers was never doubted.

Alexandra was a loving wife, devoted to Taso and she gave him confidence in everything he did. She needed only to glance at Taso and an instant smile radiated her face. Taso, when catching a glimpse of Alexandra, would often reflect on his love for her. Their love was special and rarely were they apart, except when Taso was in his boat at sea.

The couple celebrated life and were thankful for the blessings that God had bestowed upon them, and their first Thanksgiving holiday would have special meaning for them. When the morning of that day finally came, Alexandra greeted Taso coming into the kitchen where she had already begun preparation for the meal, which would be shared later in the day with Megan and Shawn... and of course, Crock.

Taso sat in his chair at the head of the table where a neatly folded napkin sat next to a cup that awaited the hot steaming coffee that Alexandra was already pouring into it. The folded napkin had become a new symbol of love that had been familiar to him. Each day Alexandra would await its return, just as Marianas had waited the return of Demetrius. Each morning he too would re-fold the napkin after breakfast and place it in his pocket as a reminder of the wife and home that awaited his return.

Alexandra moved close to Taso's side and smiled, knowing that he would be hers to share for the day, for the holiday meant that the boat would remain secured in the harbor.

"Good morning my love, did you sleep well?" and Taso replied, "I did Alex, and did you?" Then he followed by slowly placing his arms around her slim waist, and gently but firmly pressing his head into her chest.

Alexandra put the coffee pot on the table and responded by whispering to him, "Did you hear his voice?" as she paused motionless in response to his affection. "Oh yes!" he replied, "your God just told me that he knows you are awake... and yes of course, he will guide you today as he always does."

Alex held on to Taso and said, "Ah yes... he will guide all of us today." Taso shyly replied, "Even me?"

And then with a caring and loving answer, Alexandra spoke the words, "Yes, even you... and me... and the child."

For a moment, Taso didn't respond to her reply. But then, in an instant his arms released from her waist and his head withdrew from her chest as he quickly rose to his feet, staring into her eyes. He had trouble speaking as tears welled within his dark eyes as he struggled with the words. "Do you mean... do you mean what I'm hearing you say?"

Alexandra's face held the look that time had always reserved for this special moment, and her smile radiated the blessing held deep within her womb. "Yes, we're now a family, and nothing can separate us."

Taso swept Alexandra into his arms and lifted her off her feet, spinning her in a wide circle, and danced to an unheard song of joy. Then, stopping suddenly, he gently placed her down and said to her, "Oh my Alex, I must be careful not to hurt you or the baby," and he lowered his eyes to her belly and then back again into her eyes. Their bodies gently pressed against one another... and the child within her womb felt their love penetrate its own soul.

The months passed slowly leading up to the birth of their child, and Taso spoiled Alexandra with his affection. She would lovingly scold him when he tried to help her with chores, "Don't worry about me, God will take care of me, the child and this house when you are on the boat, ... go, rest!" And she would tug at Taso until he gave in to her.

Each morning Taso would hesitate at the breakfast table far longer than it would normally take for him to down the last drop of his second cup of coffee. Alexandra would remind him about her and God's agreement and insist that they would be okay. Reluctantly Taso would leave, taking the napkin with him, but have Alexandra and the child dominate his thoughts throughout the day.

Even when he worked on the boat, his mind was with his family. He often paused on the boat and would take the linen napkin out of his pocket and rub his calloused hands across its soft surface as if it were the face of his lover. He could feel the depth of their love in the symbol of the napkin and the assurance that she and the child would be there when he returned.

Taso would recall that on one cold spring morning while pulling traps along the ledge, he gasped when the cold Atlantic waters surprisingly splashed onto his face. His reaction was followed by a vision of his child being born and how it would gasp its first breath as the cold delivery room air would meet its face to tell his lungs to take in air for the first time... a survival instinct required to begin and sustain life.

He thought out loud, saying, "See, God is preparing us for the cold waters of life, but don't worry... He'll guide us," repeating those words that Alexandra spoke so often.

Each day Taso quickly and cautiously worked the trap lines during the months preceding the child's birth, but was keenly aware that any accident on the boat could affect the life of his family. At the end of the day he was always the first one back in the harbor and quickly cleaned his boat, singing one of the songs that his father would sing to him as a child.

He worked hard and with deliberate movement as he muttered to himself, "If she'll not let me scrub the kitchen floor, she can't stop me from scrubbing this one," and he would laugh to himself and sing even louder. The boat always emerged tidy and clean, followed by his traditional cleaning and clanging of the Ship's bell to announce the end of a safe workday.

It was almost a week after the expected due date for the child to be born, when on a warm summer's morning in late July, Taso emerged from his bedroom and sat at his place at the table. As usual, Alexandra greeted him with a gentle embrace, as he placed his strong arms around her protruded belly, laying his head onto her chest and asking, "Will you be okay today, or should I stay home to greet our new child?" She replied in a tone of disappointment, "You might as well go out to do what you must do, I feel far too good for a child to be born today. Anyway, Megan is coming here this morning to help me with some chores, and I'll be okay"... and together, as if choreographed they said, "And God will guide and protect me."

Together, they broke out in laughter as they shared a long embrace, sending the joy of their love into her womb where the child kicked in acceptance.

That day, Taso reluctantly left his wife and child to begin his day's work on the boat, but first he had to attend to some minor chores in and around the gear shed at home. He began by repairing some traps that would be taken out on the boat. Then, realizing that he had not checked his truck's motor oil level for some time, he opened the hood and reached in to grab the dipstick.

After all, a good mechanic would make sure that the lifeblood in the motor ran full and clean. While the engine did not need a full quart of oil, Taso decided to top it off anyway, assured that it would only take a moment to add a little oil and the engine deserved to be cared for properly.

As Taso was finishing his chores, anticipating the short drive to the dock, he saw Alexandra coming out of the back kitchen door. The expression on her face did not have that magical smile that was usually attached to it, but more so an expression of concern. The front of her dress below her waist was stained pink with liquid, as if the kitchen sink had fought back the morning chores.

Her words did not have the same confidence that they usually had, and with trembling in her voice she spoke, "My love, don't leave us, I think that our baby is coming!" Taso knew that the moment had arrived and he reached for Alexandra's arms to stabilize her movement toward him.

With deliberate but forced calm in his voice, he replied, "Alex, let's go now, the hospital is only a short drive away... can you make it okay?"

"Yes," she replied as both she and Taso moved toward the truck's passenger side where he gently helped her in.

The drive to the hospital seemed longer than it would normally take, as each bump in the road released painful groans from Alex. Taso began humming a quiet tune, one that was often sung by his father during tenuous times at sea. Glancing down to Alexandra's belly, he noticed that the pink stain had darkened to a darker red. "Don't worry Alex, God knows you are here... and He will guide us."

They soon approached the hospital and rushed in through the emergency room doors, where Alexandra had often helped when she was working there. The nurse on duty recognized Alex and glanced at the stained dress, silently revealing a look of concern on her face. "Don't worry Alex, you're in good hands now, and everything will be alright," as she helped Alexandra into a wheelchair.

In a few seconds Taso was left standing alone, as he watched Alexandra being taken away. At no other time in his life did Taso feel so helpless and alone as he watched Alexandra and his child disappear through swinging double-doors with a sign above it announcing "ONLY EMERGENCY ROOM PERSONEL PERMITTED BEYOND THIS POINT!"

Taso was never comfortable with the sterile environment of a hospital. He was used to open spaces and fresh sea air, and control of his own destiny. The hospital was so different and seemed cold, having an unnatural antiseptic smell, not like the salt air that was refreshing and welcoming.

Within these mysterious doors people moved swiftly through the halls to attend to as many needs as they could in the shortest amount of time. There was little chance that they would develop a friendship with those they met, because there was little time to do so. Alexandra was aware of this environment and was an exception to the normal rules, often developing long lasting relationships with patients, visiting them at their homes to care for them.

Even during the most critical, life threatening moments, personal relationships in the hospital would have to be put aside for patient care. Open wards would house as many patients as could be handled by a group of nurses and doctors that made rounds from bed to bed.

Privacy was something that was given up when you entered the hospital, and trust in the system was accepted as an integral part of the experience. Once you "surrendered yourself" to the realm of the hospital, you would seemingly become its property, and it controlled the path to your freedom and recovery.

Taso could not help but think that as a patient, your destiny was often clouded in the mystery of what goes on within the walls of the hospital ward. In contrast, when you were on the dock or in your boat, you were in control of your own destiny. You knew your friends and would pause to greet one another, shake hands or to talk with them about what was happening on their boat's or in their homes. Moments were never rushed, for friendShip's were too important, and your dependence on one another was life sustaining. But within the walls of the hospital, everyone seemed to perform in a pall of secrecy... talking in the strange language of medicine that was rarely understood by the patient.

A patient under stress might be left in a cloud of uncertainty, as treatments for their illness were administered, often leaving them confused and frightened. The hospital was a different world for its short-term guest, and, "You're going home" were the most welcomed words one would hear.

Alexandra had been taken from the world that she understood and was now in a world where she would have to trust others... others who held the life of her and her child within their hands.

Moments after Alex was whisked away, Taso was led to a small waiting room where several small chairs were lined up along one of the walls. Next to one of the chairs was a small table with a pile of old, well-worn magazines scattered about. The nurse attendant had instructed Taso that he would be contacted shortly about Alexandra's progress, but long hours passed with little word of her condition.

Each time that Taso would see the nurse, he would anxiously ask her about Alexandra, but her answer was always the same, and with a forced smile on her face she would reply, "She's doing fine, you know these things can take time. Just make yourself comfortable and we'll let you know when the baby comes."

Then finally, late into the evening, the nurse appeared, but this time she didn't have that forced smile on her face, it was more of a concerned look. "Well Mr. Pappas, congratulations, you are now the father of a healthy beautiful new child, and he looks just like you, and has hair just like your wife's." Taso's first words were, "Did you say he?" The nurse looked at Taso as if it were obvious what she had said, "Yes... he's a boy, and he is truly a beautiful child... as I said."

Taso was overjoyed with the news and asked, "How are

Alexandra and the baby doing?" The nurse responded with a more serious tone, "The baby is just fine and has all ten fingers and toes... and really strong lungs." As for Alex... well, she's fine, but she had a hard time and lost a little blood giving birth. But she's strong and she'll recover in no time. She's resting right now, but in a little while we'll let you see her and the baby." Taso was relieved at the news, and anxious to meet his new son and see Alexandra.

After a half hour or so, a doctor appeared through the doors of the waiting room. "Hello, Mr. Pappas, I'm Doctor Blake," as he reached for Taso's hand.

"Congratulations, you have a fine son, and he's doing just great. As for Alexandra, she's going to be okay, but she's very weak right now. She had a tough time delivering and lost a lot of blood. We think that we have the bleeding under control, but to be sure, we'll need a little more time. In the meantime, you can see Alexandra and the baby, but just for a few minutes. Then she'll need plenty of rest before we can better evaluate her recovery."

Taso responded quickly, "I want to see her and the baby right now, please take me to them." The doctor responded, "Surely, but remember, only for a few minutes, she needs her rest." "I understand," Taso answered... "Now let's go!"

Without hesitation, the doctor turned and left the waiting room while Taso followed right behind him. When they finally reached the maternity ward where Alexandra was recovering, he was surprised to see several nurses around her bed, holding her hands and whispering to one another. As he approached, the nurses parted, revealing Alexandra quietly lying in the bed with her eyes closed.

Alexandra's face was pale, and her normally soft silky hair was wet and tangled in clumps. Taso had never seen Alexandra in such a way, for she always had color and life radiating from her face, but now she looked so different.

"Alex, it's me," he whispered, as Alexandra's eyes slowly opened and met his. Her drawn, weakened face immediately showed a smile, as she struggled to speak to Taso.

"Hello Papa" she said, "We have a son, and he's so beautiful... he looks just like you." Taso wanted to hold Alexandra, but he quickly realized that she was too weak to accept his arms.

At that very moment a nurse appeared from behind him, holding their son, wrapped in a swaddling blanket. "Mr. Pappas, it's time to meet your new son," as she moved the child toward him, waiting for Taso to take the child from her. Taso didn't hesitate, and anxiously reached for the child, drawing him into his protecting arms.

Tears welled in his eyes as he looked at the baby for the first time. The child within the blanket was indeed beautiful, having dark silky hair, the same color and texture as Alexandra's. The child's face had strong features just like Taso, and his skin was smooth and clear as if he were weeks old and not just minutes old. He looked exceptionally strong as his legs kicked wildly as if he were just as excited to meet his father, as Taso was to meet him.

The child's eyes were wide open, examining his father as intently as Taso was examining him, and for a brief second the child smiled at him. Taso immediately exclaimed, "See, he already knows who I am," and everyone laughed as the fisherman lovingly held the child.

Alexandra's soft voice interrupted the moment, as she asked Taso, "What shall we call him?" Taso paused for a moment, staring at the child and answered as if he always knew that the child would be born a boy. "Michael... we shall call him Michael... after the Archangel that God had chosen as the most trusted protector of man."

Alexandra's smile confirmed her pleasure at the chosen name, as Taso placed the child into her arms and then kissed her cheek, saying, "You have given me the greatest gift that I have ever received, and I'll love and take care of him forever."

Alex was at peace holding the child, and having Taso now with her, but she was showing signs of discomfort. Dr. Blake quickly spoke, "I think that we should give Alexandra and the baby... I mean Michael, some rest now. You can come back later to see both of them."

Taso knew that Alexandra needed rest, and surely he would come back to see them. He bent low, placing a kiss on Alexandra's cheek, and with his thumb, made the sign-of-the-cross on Michael's forehead. Then he kissed Michael's forehead and smiled at them both, saying, "You are in good hands," knowing that what he meant went beyond the care of the nurses and Dr. Blake.

Hope for the future was now their strength, and new life would begin, not as Taso and Alexandra, but now as the Pappas family.

Each day thereafter, Taso visited Alex and Michael, but their shared dreams were interrupted when it was discovered that something of grave concern was happening to Alexandra. During the birthing process, Alexandra began to lose blood. At first it seemed not to be a big concern, and Dr. Blake began to initiate procedures to stop the bleeding. There was little response to the effort, and the bleeding continued until a few days later when Alexandra's strength began to dwindle.

Dr. Blake and the hospital team were doing everything possible to try to stop the uncontrolled bleeding, but very little seemed to work as they frantically attended to Alexandra.

Alexandra's body was rapidly weakening so that she was no longer able to breast feed Michael, her strength diminishing to the point that she slipped into a partial state of coma several times. Only for brief moments did she awaken, always calling for Taso and Michael.

During the days that followed, close friends visited Alexandra, but were never actually able to communicate with her. Crock even stopped by to bring Michael a small, carved scrimshaw dolphin that looked very real. But Crock never stayed very long because of his discomfort with hospital spaces.

Megan and Shawn were there almost as often as Taso, only going home at night. When they were there, Megan would hold Michael in her arms, giving him as much attention as Alexandra would have.

Megan would feed Michael from a bottle, holding him close to her own body, as she too longed for the blessings of having a child. For several years Shawn and Megan had tried to have children, but eventually learned that they might never be able to do so. They loved children, and had been earlier asked to be Godparents to Michael when he was to be baptized.

For Megan, the presence of Michael in her life was cherished because of her deep love for Alexandra and Taso. She would do anything for Alexandra, and Alexandra would do anything for her.

During the silent moments when Alex slept, Taso would talk to Megan and Shawn about his love for Alexandra. He told them the story of their first encounter on the *Eagles Wing's*, and how the special locket was lost when it snagged on a trap, and how they vowed that nothing ever again could separate their love.

Word of Alexandra's condition rapidly passed through the village, and everyone was stunned at the disturbing news. Crock would come to the hospital every day, but would not enter the ward where his friends sat alongside of Alexandra. Instead, he would pace the halls, hobbling back and forth on his bad leg, until Taso would come out and convince him that everything was going to be okay.

Reluctantly Crock would leave, but always instructing Taso, "Ya just make sure that ya gives her and the baby a hug from me when ya see them again." Then he would slowly turn and leave the hall, with his head bowed low.

On the third day following Michael's birth, Taso was alone, holding Michael while faithfully keeping watch over his beloved Alexandra. Dr. Blake appeared at the entrance to the ward, assisted by several Interns.

The doctor immediately moved toward Taso and began speaking with concern and uncertainty in his voice. "Mr. Pappas, we're not able to stop the bleeding, and Alexandra is in very critical condition. We've tried everything, but nothing seems to work. I'm afraid that she can't survive much longer. We're trying to make her comfortable, but that's about all we can do for her. I'm afraid that at her rate of decline, she only has a few days at best before her systems shut down completely... I'm very sorry."

Taso knew that Alexandra was in serious condition, but he didn't expect to hear what the doctor had just told him. His heart sank in confusion as he spoke with denial in his voice,

"This can't be happening to her, she's a strong woman, and it's only childbirth... why is this happening... why isn't the bleeding stopping... isn't there anything else you can do?"

The doctor continued to look at Taso, and with concerned sadness in his voice, he answered, "No Mr. Pappas, I'm sorry, but there is nothing else we can do, she's in God's hands now."

This is not what Taso wanted to hear, as tears welled in his eyes, and turning toward Alexandra, he finally began to realize the seriousness of the situation.

While Taso had seen death before, and saved many men's lives while in the heat of battle during the war, he would be brought to the brink of hell as he watched his beloved struggling for her life... and not being able to do anything about it.

The normally strong, confident sea Captain now felt helpless and alone in this battle, and could only watch as Alexandra silently lay there. Taso never left her side, always holding her hand and whispering stories of what he had done on the boat, or anything that he felt she might hear in her silent sleep. Sometimes he would quietly hum a Greek tune to her while holding Michael, as they sat close to her, watching for some sign that she might get better.

Only once did it appear that Alexandra was responding. For a brief second, her eyes opened slightly as her head turned toward Michael, and she reached out to touch him. Exhaustion interrupted the attempt, as her hand dropped to the bed and she slipped back into sleep.

Taso continually prayed to God to allow her to open her eyes, if even for only a moment so that if she saw him or Michael, perhaps her spirits would be lifted. But her eyes remained closed throughout the day.

The days went on with no progress, as doctors and nurses constantly changed dressings and tried to comfort her. She was weakening far too quickly, and her normally radiant face was now drawn and colorless.

Taso never left Alexandra's side, constantly caressing her and whispering his love for her.

Watching Alex in this way was painful and confusing to Taso, as he watched her strength slowly leave her body. He would pray quietly to himself... "God, please guide and protect her today."

Several times he would nod off for a few seconds, dreaming of images of Michael feeling the warmth of Alexandra's breast, as the child would receive life-giving nourishment from her body. But this would not be the case, for she was fighting to maintain her own life, and she would not feel the warmth of Michael's face on her breast.

On the morning of the fifth day after Michael's birth, Taso was once again sitting at Alexandra's side and holding Michael. A nurse had just finished checking Alexandra's condition, and when she finished, she left the room... uncharacteristically not looking at Taso.

Taso continued to stare at Alex, and noticed that her face was somehow different than before. Was it the morning sunrise that was peeking through the window, sending its warm glow across her face? Then, his attention was drawn to a slight movement coming from Alexandra's hand.

Alexandra's head turned toward her Captain as she fought to slowly open her eyes. Taso was startled to see his beautiful Alexandra, as a weak smile appeared on her face. She reached toward Taso's hand where it met her hand, and with a gentle squeeze acknowledged their presence.

Taso could see that Alexandra was trying to speak, but was having trouble doing so. He quickly whispered to her, so that she would not have to struggle, "We're here my love." But Taso felt a strain in his soul, as fear shook his body.

He could see the approach of death on her face, but he fought every emotion to not let her see him in a troubled way.

Then, Alexandra let go of Taso's hand and moved it onto Michael's small body, stroking the child's face... and looking into Taso's eyes, she struggled to whisper the words that he would never forget.

"I give to you this son, Michael... out of my deepest love for you. Love him and guide him... teach him that God's peace replaces all fear." Then, all too quickly her eyes closed for the last time... and she was silent.

Taso pleaded, "No... Alex... Alex please don't go," but nothing that he could say would bring her back, as shocked realization filled the fisherman's eyes with tears. His head slowly sank down toward Alexandra... for he and Michael were now alone.

Taso's sobbing brought attention to the nurses on duty, and they silently entered the room. Not far behind them came Megan and Shawn who quickly knew what had happened. Megan rushed to the bedside where she placed her hands on Alexandra's motionless shoulders, and began to weep bitterly at the loss of her best friend. Shawn stopped behind Taso and Michael, silently making his presence known to them.

After what seemed to be a long time, but was only a few minutes, Taso's last gesture to Alex was to lift Michael up and place the baby in her arms so that he would feel the warmth of her body for one last time. A gentle smile remained on Alexandra's face as Michael softly cooed in her lifeless arms.

Then after a few minutes, Taso reached for Michael, lifting him back into his arms, leaving Alexandra in peace.

The only sound that followed was the distant pealing of a small ship's bell, wailing in protest in the harbor... and Michael's cry for the breast of his mother, which would never again be offered to comfort him.

For Taso, the uncertain future was filled with confusion and pain as unanswered questions of "why" constantly filled his being.

The funeral services following Alexandra's death were held in the same church where the couple had first met, and was attended by practically the whole village. The loss for Taso and Michael would be monumental, and the community would never again have such a loving and caring steward.

After the church services ended, Alexandra would be put to rest in the small cemetery where Taso, years ago, had puzzled over the tombstone epitaph of a young Ship's Master. Now, and many times to come, he would visit this gravesite and look upon Alexandra's tombstone... puzzling over the untimely death of the person he most loved in the world, and he would once again puzzle over the question of "why?"

Chapter Twelve

During the time following Alexandra's death, there was little occasion for Taso to grieve his loss, as he struggled to learn all he could about raising a baby and maintaining the livelihood of a lobsterman... both tasks requiring all the patience, strength and attention possible. He often relied on two of his closest friends for help and guidance.

Although Megan and Shawn Foster didn't have children of their own, their love for little Michael became an outlet for sharing their own love. When it came time to baptize Michael, Megan and Shawn were prepared to honor Alex and Taso's previous invitation to become Michael's godparents.

A warm Sunday morning in August found Taso walking the path toward the church where the baptism would take place. In his arms he held the peacefully sleeping Michael wearing a white silk gown that made him indistinguishable as a boy. Megan had made the special gown from pieces of the dress that Alexandra wore during her wedding.

Earlier that morning, Taso baffled at how to put the gown on Michael, all the while cautiously trusting that the feminine looking wardrobe that Megan made, was proper for the occasion.

Across Taso's shoulder was his old Navy duffle bag, containing milk and soft cloth diapers if needed for the child throughout the morning. Taso had chosen to walk the path because he wanted Michael to feel the warm morning sun on his face, and breathe the fresh sea air into his lungs.

As they reached the familiar stone bench where Taso and Alexandra often embraced and shared their dreams, he paused and sat for a moment, whispering softly to the sleeping child in his arms, "My child, this day you will receive a special gift... a gift that will become your strength. Your mother, Alexandra, possessed this same gift, and she would want you to have it also. It is a most powerful gift... one that will protect you throughout life's most demanding challenges. You will learn the power of the gift, and will always be safe when you put your trust in it."

At the conclusion of his words, Michael's eyes began to open as he looked up to his father's face and smiled... as if he had heard every word that Taso spoke. Taso reacted by bending his head down toward the baby's face, and gently kissing his cheek, saying, "I see that when I speak your mother's name, you are awakened, and feel her spirit." Michael responded to the kiss by closing his eyes and resuming his peaceful sleep.

Taso then got up, turned toward the path leading to the church and whispered again to Michael, "We'd better go now, Father Benning, Megan and Shawn will be at Saint Finbarr's, waiting to celebrate your gift."

When Taso and Michael arrived at the church, Father Benning, Megan and Shawn were already there to greet them. With an anxious smile on her face, Megan instinctively reached for the baby and began to talk to him as if the sleeping Michael could hear what she was saying, "Oh my precious little baby... just look at you. You look so beautiful in your gown." But before she could finish her praises, Taso looked at Shawn, and Shawn stared back at Taso, both shrugging their shoulders while Taso jokingly whispered, "He looks like a girl in that gown... shouldn't he be wearing pants... or maybe oilskins?"

At that, Shawn tried to hold back a laugh, but Megan's strained look back toward him quickly set the seriousness of the mood, and he nervously coughed to clear his throat... now showing proper acceptance of the gown. Megan then continued her praises, "He looks like an angel in his gown," and Taso was not about to challenge her words.

Father Benning was anxious to begin in what was to be his first Baptismal ceremony, and spoke proudly, "What a magnificent day you've chosen for Michael's baptism... the sun is shining brightly," as he gestured toward the stained glass window over Saint Finbarr's doors, where brilliant sunlight was piercing through an image of a dove... sending its reflected image on the floor where Megan stood holding Michael. He then continued, "We should begin now... so everyone, please take your places around the baptismal font.

"Megan, you'll be holding Michael just as you are... and Shawn, you'll stand next to Megan. Mr. Pappas, you stand on the other side of Megan and Michael."

When everything seemed in order, they were ready to begin, as Father Benning opened his "Book of Cannon Rite for Baptism". He spoke to Megan and Shawn first, explaining, "I will be asking Michael for responses to the rite of baptism. You, being his godparents," and then looking toward Taso he continued, "and you, his father... will respond for Michael."

The three acknowledged by nodding their heads together in acceptance as the ceremony was about to begin.

Then Father Benning began the ritual by first making the sign of the cross with his right hand and saying, "We gather here in the name of the Father, and of the Son, and of the Holy Ghost... Amen. Dear friends, you have brought this child to the presence of the Holy One, to receive the waters of baptism. May these waters bring him a purity of heart and new life as we ask for this blessing upon these waters." Then Father Benning blessed the waters within the font and preceded on with the ceremony, asking, "What name do you give this child?" Taso responded, "Michael."

****

Outside of the Chapel, facing west toward the steep rock cliff where the black stripe markings characterized the name of Black Point Cove, the seas began to swell and churn over the black rocks scattered along its shore... even though the sun continued to shine and no wind was present.

After a moment of prayer over the waters, Father Benning proceeded on to the ritual prayers of atonement and renunciation of Satan, as his voice took a serious tone. It was now that Taso, Megan and Shawn would be asked to speak for Michael, as Father Benning would direct the questions toward them.

"Michael, do you reject sin so as to live in the freedom of God's children?" the Priest asked loudly, somewhat startling the participants, as he paused for them to respond.

"Yes... we do reject sin," was their swift reply.

****

The seas along the black rock cliff began to protest wildly as waves pounded against the rocks below sent vertical plumes of murky water skyward. Nowhere in the Cove, except at the base of the black rock did the mood of the sea change from still blue water to agitated dark iridescent churning waves.

****

"Do you reject the glamour of evil and refuse to be mastered by sin?" the Priest proclaimed even louder than before... again waiting for a reply. "Yes... we do reject the glamour of sin and refuse to be mastered by it!" came the reply.

****

Turbulent, almost frozen slushy iridescent waters spiraled up the black rock, as if an evil force were regurgitating the cold mass upward, ripping sharp chunks of stone from its face and thrusting them against the sheer cliff where they broke into jagged pieces and tumbled haphazardly back to the shore below.

****

"Do you reject Satan, father of sin and prince of darkness?"

The priest once again pleaded, as beads of perspiration began to form on his forehead. "Yes... we do reject Satan, father of sin and prince of darkness!" was the resounding reply from Michael's father and godparents.

****

Continuing below the black cliffs, foaming thick waves rose upward in geyser-like fashion and belched cold ink-black water and shards of rock in an endless display of repugnance. As the dark water spilled over the cliff, it left frozen ice formations resembling sharp black incisors dangling from the jagged rocks.

****

The ritual continued as Father Benning responded, "You have proclaimed for Michael, his intent to be baptized in the faith of the Church" The priest placed his cupped hands into the baptismal font, scooping water into them, and proceeded to pour it over Michael's head, saying, "I baptize you in the name of the Father... and reaching again into the font for more water, again pouring it over Michael's head saying, "And of the Son... and for a final draw of water, once more pouring over the child's head, "And of the Holy Ghost... Amen!"

****

The turbulent cold sea below the black rock sent its last violent plume skyward, almost reaching the top of the cliff... sending a thunderous explosive roar that echoed across the cove. At the opposite side of the cove, startled villagers strolling the shore turned their heads toward the cliff to see what the noise was all about, but by the time they focused on it, everything was over.

****

As the last drops of Holy Water spilled off of Michael's head, he awakened from his sleep and smiled upward toward his father. Across Michael's chest emerged the radiant glowing reflected image of a dove, being projected from the stained glass window overhead.

The gift that his father had promised to Michael... had been received.

Within the small church, Baptism had brought the promise of peace and protection to the child... but outside of the holy place, the turbulent cold waters along the black rock shore rushed to subside into calm smooth surf, as frozen incisors hanging from the jagged surfaces quickly melted, leaving ebony streaks on the rock's face.

Peace too, had now been brought back to nature, as gentle waves spilled calmly over the black rocks along the shore.

A small child had received a gift that would change the course of the lives of everyone he would encounter, and those who loved him most would be forever changed by his presence.

Days, weeks and months passed after the baptism of Michael, and Megan cared for the child daily when Taso was working on his boat. Megan loved Michael as if he was her own child, and Michael grew close to her as they shared special moments together.

Megan would feed him, bathe him and attend to all of his needs. She would read stories to him, placing him on a quilted blanket on the floor, the same place where his father often played with Michael. Shawn also, grew close to Michael and loved him dearly, like a caring uncle to him.

Since Megan was an accomplished seamstress, she would often make special outfits for Michael. One particular garment was made to resemble the sailor suit that Taso wore when he was in the Navy.

Taso would often dress Michael in the "cute sailor suit," as Megan put it, and then place the little sailor on his shoulders to parade him around the dock. Taso would approach everyone, telling them that his son would someday become a great fisherman... like him.

Taso was patiently learning how to be a father, and leapt at every chance to try something new... as long as it involved Michael. He was especially aware of the softer elements of life that typically involved a woman's touch. Alexandra had introduced these soft elements to Taso, but she wouldn't be there when Michael needed them. So, Taso awkwardly tried to introduce them to Michael, usually taking guidance from Megan.

Taso would often sing to Michael while swinging him in his arms. His favorite thing to do was to place Michael in the middle of the floor on a quilted blanket, and dance a traditional Greek *choros dance* in circles around him. Michael would never loose eye contact with his father, twisting his head as far as it would go around, and then turning sharply back to catch his father's movements on the other side of the animated circle. Music and dancing were a special part of their lives, and every chance Taso had, he would be clapping hands high over his head, and teaching Michael the words to many classical Greek songs.

Michael always smiled his mother's smile and watched his father when he danced and sang. It didn't matter if there was music or not... the dance and songs were more important than the music, and the dancer more important than the song or dance itself.

Taso also inherited the gift of storytelling, something he learned from his own father. He would make up dramatic stories about things that a fisherman might understand, like boat's and the sea, or creatures within it.

It didn't matter what the subject was, for the story was a way for them to communicate and their spirits to bond. No matter what the story was about, it would be filled with drama and excitement that a child would instinctively learn lessons of life and love.

Occasionally Taso would revert to one of the more traditional tales about little pigs or animals living in the woods, often changing the outcome to meet the storyteller's mood. After all, stories were just that, stories, and the outcome needed to be flexible for a child's imagination to develop.

Almost everything Taso said to Michael somehow ended in a story. Michael loved the sound of his father's voice, and would stare at him in a trance-like state, hanging onto every word as Taso wove one of his tales. There was little silence in the house when the two were present, either Taso was talking to Michael, or Michael was babbling on to his Papa. Music coming from records played on an old "Victrola" became the background for their song and dance, as its sound reverberated through open windows out to the sea.

Often the story or dance ended with both Michael and his father laughing in each other's arms. As Michael grew, he repeated the songs almost perfectly, but occasionally inserted a new word where there was one that he couldn't say. When Michael learned to walk, well before he was a year old, he immediately tried to mimic the *choros dance* as Taso had done, but often fell to the floor crying... only to be retrieved into the protective arms of his father to comfort him.

Perseverance overcame time and little Michael's determined legs grew strong, allowing him to dance and twirl far too quickly for such a little boy. Sometimes he would spin in circles so fast and so many times that he became dizzy and toppled to the floor out of control. Both Michael and Taso laughed when this happened and often ended up as before, hugging in a silent and loving embrace.

Michael needed Taso as much as Taso needed Michael and rarely were they beyond eye site of one another except when Taso was at sea. It was then that Megan's love would pacify the child as she cared for him during the long days when Taso worked the boat. But the moment that Taso entered their home to reclaim his son, Michael's scurried leap into his father's arms would once again bring oneness to the pair.

Michael grew from toddler into early childhood, all the while developing a deep personal love for nature and the sea. Under the watchful eye of Taso or Megan, he loved to play at the shoreline, studying any object or creature that emerged from its depths. If a creature were injured, he would try to heal it and often kept it in an empty fish storage box just out of reach from the tides. He would fill the box with seaweed and water and then care for little crabs, snails or starfish until they were healed. Eventually these creatures would be released back into the sea, but only when Michael thought they were strong enough.

Michael often would search the sky for seabirds, and marvel at their ability to soar and dive toward the water, snatching unwary fish for a meal. He would ponder at how a gull or Osprey could stay motionless a hundred feet in the air, wings spread open and balancing effortlessly on the wind currents overhead. And like his mother, he too would be deeply saddened by the loss of any creature, often asking his father, "Papa, why do things have to die?" And Taso would again struggle at answering the question, "It's the way of life I suppose," he would answer... but never with a very convincing voice.

At times when Taso would bring him on the boat, Michael would follow him around, always being at his side and asking question-after-question about what he was doing. Michael liked to touch everything and would often ask, "Papa... can I help do this or that?" But the usual answer would be; "Not yet Michael, this is very dangerous and you could get hurt, but perhaps when you're bigger."

Usually Taso would let Michael untangle the warp lines used on his traps, and Michael pursued the task as if it were the most important thing to do on the boat. He could spend hours meticulously untangling the lines, rarely asking Taso for help. When he was finished, he would wind the warps in perfect loops on the deck, and look up at Taso exclaiming in victory, "Look Papa, I did it!" And Taso would always answer back, "Yes my little fisherman, you did it," making sure that Michael knew that he had done the task well.

Michael's emerging love for every form of life would follow him wherever he would go. And while Taso was overjoyed at how Michael was growing, and the love between them, he longed for Alexandra's love, often visioning her and Michael together in his dreams.

He dreamed of seeing Alexandra pushing Michael on a swing, laughing as Michael squealed out, "Higher Mama, go very high!" Sometimes he would dream of seeing her holding Michael, while she sang a lullaby as Michael slept peacefully, cooing in her arms. But always the dreams would end too soon; waking him up to the reality that she wasn't there.

Not a day passed when Taso would stop to reflect on his love for Alexandra, often while staring out from the bay window on the home that they built together. He would see the stone seat along the path, and recall their times together, dreaming of what life would bring to them, but never realizing how short their life together would be. But there would be little time for reflection, for Michael's needs almost always drew Taso away from the window and back into Michael's own little world.

Michael was growing in strength, knowledge and grace, as he approached the wise-old-age of five, when he entered kindergarten, and befriended everyone in his class. His teachers would often comment on how Michael seemed to calm other classmates who might be a little unruly.

In no time he advanced to the first, and then second grades. He was usually the first person to make friends with the other children, and always protected the smaller ones from those who were more aggressive, for he was a peacemaker, like his father was.

Michael learned quickly, and never feared trying something new. When he didn't understand something, he would ask questions until they were answered to his own satisfaction... everyone often commenting about him; "How is it that this child of such a young age has such wisdom and patience... he is so different from the other children?"

When his class was singing songs, Michael sang the loudest and with the clearest voice, honed by the practice of singing classical Greek tunes learned at home. When he and his father would dance in their living room, he danced with agility and never missed a step. And when he played games, he played by the rules and laughed the loudest. To his teachers and playmates, Michael was a role model, and they were always aware of his presence and wanted to be with him.

Michael was growing up to be a lot like his father, patient and resourceful, never to waste anything... and sensitive to the needs of others, just like his mother had been. He was determined in everything he did, but always willing to change his direction if it was the best thing to do.

When Taso would help Shawn at the repair shop, Michael would play with the tools, often mimicking their actions, by banging on a piece of equipment as if he were fixing it.

As he grew older, he would be allowed to take apart discarded broken parts, spending hours trying to disassemble and reassemble them. When it was time to leave the shop, he would reluctantly stop what he was doing, and remind them; "Okay, but don't touch this, I'm going to finish it tomorrow," and tomorrow he did.

Taso marveled at Michael's ability to persevere through the most complex tasks, often getting so involved into something that he completely was unaware of time or anything around him.

When Megan would bake cakes and cookies in her kitchen, Michael was often planted at her side, carefully measuring flour or other ingredients. He would emerge with more flour on him than would end up in the mixing bowls. But when all was done and the baked goods emerged from the hot oven, he would parade around with a tray of treats, exclaiming to everyone, "look, I helped make these!"

Michael gave to others his magic personality and seemed to bring peace and harmony wherever he was. He also inherited the unusual quality of being both gentle and strong, just as Taso had learned from Alexandra. Michael knew how to celebrate life. One moment he could be chattering away to himself or singing a song, or dancing about in deliberate steps to the unheard sounds of music. Then, a moment later, as quickly as he started dancing, he could stop and quietly direct his complete attention to the land or sea around him.

Michael also found solace on the stone bench where his mother and father had dreamed their dreams. He would pause to reflect on the mysterious call of the gulls or the pounding surf at the edge of their property, where waves advanced and then retreated in an endless motion hour-after-hour, day-after-day.

The young child Michael, studied the creatures of the sea and would ponder... where did all the water come from and where did it go several times a day? The shore and ocean were Michael's natural home, but he was at his happiest when his father took him on the boat.

When on board the boat, Taso assumed the role of the Captain of the ship, putting aside his fatherly role... for the sea could be brutal and leadership was necessary for survival.

Michael was allowed to do small chores on the boat, but always under the Captain's watchful eye. One time Taso was testing the limits of what Michael might do on the boat, and he asked him to sort through the bait barrel for bad bait. This was the most disgusting chore on a lobster boat, even for a seasoned Sternman. The ripe bait, usually fish heads, was necessary for the traps, but after a point if the bait decayed too much, the lobsters wouldn't take it. So from time-to-time, the bad bait had to be separated from the usable bait.

The way this was done was by putting on rubber gloves and reaching into the barrel and searching until you found the decaying squishy bad bait, and then usually throwing it overboard. Michael was familiar with the bait barrel, for he often peered into it, examining the lifeless forms within it, trying to imagine what it would look like if it were alive.

Taso initiated the challenge by saying, "Michael, I have a very important job that I want you to do." Michael's response was quick and attentive, "Yes Papa, what can I do?" The Captain then patiently instructed him, saying, "I want you to sort through the bait barrel and throw out the rotten bait."

"Okay Papa, I can do that!" Michael answered, while turning his head toward the bait barrel. Taso removed a rubber glove that he was wearing, and handed it to him.

Michael never thought twice about accepting this new job, and struggled to put the oversized glove onto his small hand. It was all that Taso could do to keep from laughing at the sight of Michael with the large rubber glove flopping around on his hand.

Without hesitation, Michael approached the bait barrel and looked into it, surveying the task at hand. With his left hand he pinched off his nose, and with his right hand ready for action, plunged it into the barrel and began to sort through the slimy mess. Michael patiently probed around the pieces of bait, pushing aside the firm pieces and searching deeper inside for the bad ones.

Taso watched in surprise as Michael searched the smelly bait without hesitation. Then to his surprise, Michael pulled his gloved hand from the barrel, holding a mass of decayed bait. "Look, I found some!" he exclaimed, as if he had discovered gold. "What should I do with it?" He asked, still pinching off his nose with his free hand.

Taso was just as surprised as Michael was, but for a different reason. Taso was seeing Michael do something that even a seasoned fisherman balked at... and Michael was not complaining about it.

Taso replied as if nothing unusual was happening, "Okay Michael, throw it overboard, we will not need that piece." Michael responded by throwing the slimy mass overboard... and immediately a gull swooped down to retrieve it. Michael smiled at the resourceful gull, proud that he was feeding one of the creatures that he so admired. And Taso reflected back to that day when Alexandra was moved to tears at the sight of an urchin being snatched up by a gull.

Remarkably, Michael spent the next half hour or so finishing the task, each time watching, as gulls approached to take the discarded bait. Michael was not seeing the task as one of disgust, but more so as a feeding opportunity for the gulls. Taso just stood back in admiration of his son, and smiled, shaking his head back and forth.

When the day was done, Michael always looked forward to helping the Captain clean the boat for the next day's work, just as he had often done at school when helping his teacher tidy the classroom for the next day.

Sometimes the Captain would allow Michael to do the one special job that signaled the end of the workday, and that was to polish the Ship's bell. This would require the ritualistic process involving a special storage box and cleaning supplies.

Usually the Captain would begin the preparation and then hand Michael the soft cloth with polish on it. Michael would approach his job much the same as he did when caring for the creatures being nursed back to health. He loved looking at the intricately molded bell as he polished it, for each time he discovered a new or different creature that was molded into its surface. He would say to his father, "Papa, I never saw this Hippo before, where do Hippo's live?" And Taso would launch into a story about Hippo's. Then the next time, Michael would discover a different animal, and once again a story would unfold.

Michael always worked in a purposeful fashion for as long as it took for the bell to emerge shining like gold, without a speck of salt or blemish on it.

Afterward, the cloth was returned back to its storage box and Michael stepped back awaiting the Captain's inspection. In jeweler-like fashion, the Captain's eyes would slowly circle the bell, side-to-side, and top to bottom, not missing a spot.

When the inspection was complete, the Captain would carefully grab the end of the bell rope, while mischievously glancing back to Michael, whom in anticipation would now have his hands cupped over his ears... eyes wide open. Then, with a quick snap of his wrist, the rope was pulled downward, sending the bell's penetrating sound resonating across the Cove.

At the moment the "ding-ding" sound emerged from the bell,

gulls went flying uncontrollably in every direction. Michael and Taso would laugh hysterically as they watched the confused gulls disappear over the horizon.

Then, as quickly as the laughing began, the Captain would quiet himself and respectfully whisper, "Let the sounds of man and nature never be silenced." Michael would look on as his father spoke those words, but in spite of all his abilities, he could not understand what it all meant. Nonetheless, he knew that they had special meaning, because the Captain was speaking them... and that alone was enough to satisfy his concern.

Chapter Thirteen

Summer in July along the New England coast is the best time of the year. No longer will the woolen jackets be required to take the chill away from even the best of late spring or early summer days. July days always seemed longer than at any other time, and after fishing all day, there was still time available to spend with family.

It was one of these special July mornings that found the Captain and Michael approaching the dock where the *Eagles Wing's* awaited their arrival. The warm morning sun greeted them in a silent explosion of bright yellow-orange and purple colors. Michael was half skipping along the wooden dock when he observed a small crab crawling up a dock post, and as usual, he stopped to see what it was doing.

Taso was walking ahead of Michael toward the *Eagles Wing's*, and upon seeing the sunrise colors, was struck by its beauty. The Captain's memory flashed back to a similar morning years ago when in the arms of his bride these same colors spoke to them a promise of new life and eternal love. His mind drifted to that Thanksgiving morning when Alexandra told him that they would always be a family and nothing could separate the three of them... but there were only two on the dock this morning.

Taso's heart began to sink as he once again longed for Alexandra's presence. How long Taso was dwelling in these past memories could not be determined, but it was soon interrupted by Michael's voice. "Papa look, this crab has a barnacle on its shell and it doesn't even know it."

Taso realized that his eyes were moist and reached into his pocket where a worn, folded linen napkin awaited his calloused hands. He wiped his eyes with it and then quickly turned his head toward Michael, knowing that he would have to postpone his moment of recollection to a later time. When his eyes met Michael's, he could see that Michael was staring back at him with concern on his little face. Michael had a special sensitivity towards other person's feelings, and would usually stop what he was doing to show his concern for others.

"Papa" he said, "is something wrong?" While Taso thought to himself... yes there is something very wrong with this situation, he knew that he shouldn't trouble the boy with his feelings, and answered, "No son, nothing's wrong, I just got a piece of dirt in my eye, but I think it's gone now." He paused momentarily, then continued, "and now it is time to move on," meaning more than just going out to sea.

What made this day special for Taso was something more important than having a reoccurring memory of Alexandra. It was now Michael's twelfth birthday, and one that would become special for both of them.

The progressing sunrise illuminated the clear blue sky hinting that this would be a fine day at sea, and he and Michael were ready to board the boat. Taso slid on his black rubber deck boots and stepped onto the boat to begin the day's work.

Michael followed by leaping over the rail in an effortless move, turning in mid-air and dropping his feet to the deck, as his bottom-side planted him squarely onto the engine cover. The Captain smiled and shook his head, thinking how nice it would be if he were that agile again. Taso then headed for the wheelhouse where he reached for his oilskin pants that would keep him dry during the morning fishing expedition. For generations, fishermen relied on their oilskins as much as any other piece of gear on a fishing boat, for they would resist the cold penetration of the Atlantic waters.

The father and son team continued to prepare the boat by placing several traps at the stern where they would be used later to replace damaged ones. Michael, who had already put on the rubber gloves and checked for over-ripe bait, completed the inspection of the bait bucket and had moved on to tend to some loose warp lines.

Finally, several long warp lines were placed in neat circular spools on the deck, to use later in the day. The boat was now ready for fishing, except for one last thing, as Taso called to Michael from the wheelhouse.

"My son, come here, we have to do one more thing before we go," Michael turned toward his father and approached him with a look of confusion on his face. "Yes Papa, what is it?"

Taso smiled at the boy and turned toward the ornately trimmed brass storage box that housed the polishing supplies, and reached in, pulling out a strange bundle wrapped in brown paper.

Around the bundle was white twine circling in each direction and tied into a loose knot at the top. Handing it to Michael, Taso said with a smile, "Happy Birthday my son, I hope you like this, it will become a part of who you are."

Michael's eyes opened wide as he moved toward his father and slowly reached toward the mysterious package. "A present for me Papa... what is it?" he exclaimed with his eye's wide open. Taso smiled back at Michael and answered, "I'm sure that if your mother were here, she would insist that you have this." This only confused Michael, for his father rarely mentioned Alexandra to him.

However, Michael had often thought about his mother, more so as he had gotten older, especially after hearing other children talk about their parents. There were times when he watched other children at school greet their mothers with a hug and a kiss, and wished he could know the intimacy of such an encounter.

While Megan often greeted Michael with a hug after school,

everyone knew that she was not his mother. Michael had never doubted his father's love for him, for he was often embraced by Taso's strong arms and kissed on the forehead or cheeks, but somehow he could not associate this with the motherly love that he had observed with his friends.

The Captain's voice interrupted Michael's reflection on the woman whose spirit bonded all three together, "Go ahead and open it before the lobsters head for deeper water on this warm day."

Michael slowly tugged at the string until it slipped open and freed the brown paper. Then he spread the paper apart to reveal its contents. He seemed even more confused as he gazed into the loose wrappings to try to understand what was inside.

It was yellow in color... smooth like a dolphin's skin, and shiny with red leather straps and shiny brass buckles.

Taso quickly realized that Michael had no idea what it was and gently reached for the package and said, "Let me help you." He removed the paper from the mystery item, and then with each hand reached for corners and quickly snapped the item forward just as he would do with sheets after being dried on a clothesline.

Magically, a small pair of yellow oilskin pants appeared, just like the ones Taso had just put on himself. "They're for me!" Michael squealed as he reached for the pants and placed them in front of his hips, as if to check that they would fit properly. "Yes my son, they're yours, and they'll bring you comfort and protection... and hopefully good luck as you become a fisherman."

Michael's broad smile confirmed his joy at receiving the gift, as he slipped each leg into the oilskins, struggling when his shoes jammed in the bottom opening. "No, my son, you must remove your shoes before putting them on... but first," then Taso paused to reach once again into the brass trimmed box and pulled out a small pair of rubber boots. "These will work properly with the pants." As fast as Michael could do so, he backed off the oilskins, removed his shoes and slid his legs easily through. Then he slipped each foot into the boots and stood up, and planted his fists on his hips to present himself to the Captain for inspection.

"How do I look Papa?" Taso was astonished at seeing his son facing him, with his hands on his hips, exactly like Alexandra once did long ago.

Taso's mind once again flashed back to that day when Alexandra spoke those exact words... when she too put on her first pair of oilskins.

With tears in his eyes, Taso was seeing and feeling the soul of Alexandra present in Michael's body. Taso moved toward Michael and wrapped his arms around his shoulders; saying, "You look like you're ready to fish," holding Michael for a long time, as the spirits of three fishermen now occupied the boat.

A moment later Taso ended the embrace, saying, "Okay now, let's get this boat moving to open waters where the lobsters are waiting for us." Michael wasn't sure what had taken place in his father's mind, but he could feel his father's love as he responded back to him, "Thank you Papa, now I'm a real fisherman... just like you... let's go."

The boat and the fishermen were now ready to depart as Taso took one last look around to make sure that everything was in order. He nodded to Michael, as if to say that everything was okay, and then headed to the pilothouse to begin the thirty-minute ride to the ledge where the traps awaited their release from the cold bottom of the ocean.

The engine was started and the captain signaled with a second nod toward Michael, indicating for him to hold on before he put the boat in motion to begin their short journey. Then Taso reached for the bell cord and gave it a snap downward, announcing the beginning of the day's work. The gearshift was placed in its proper position, and the boat gently moved forward, its one-cylinder engine "putt putting" smoothly as it made its way out of the harbor.

Michael instantly stood up and headed toward the bow of the boat so that he'd easily be seen by the other lobstermen readying their boat's for the day's work.

Proudly looking on was Taso... and if the other lobstermen were not looking back, he would ring the Ship's bell, "ding, ding," introducing the little fisherman wearing his new yellow oilskins and black boots... just like all true fishermen wore.

Smiles and waves were returned as the *Eagles Wing's* glided past the break wall and headed out toward the ledge where the day's work would begin.

The sun had finally cleared the horizon, mixing and balancing its warmth with the cool ocean breeze. The two fishermen with their bright oilskin pants and black rubber boots stood proudly as the little boat cut through the smooth blue waters of the eastern part of the cove.

As expected, thirty minutes later the colorful boat approached its destination along a shoal that ended at a steep drop off known as the ledge. This was home for Taso's lobster traps, and he knew the spot well, marked by the granite monolith praying hands pointing upward on a cliff a few hundred yards toward land. Colored buoys bobbed carelessly on top of the blue gray waters hinting of the treasures that might be attached three or four fathoms below the boat.

As the boat slowed, the Captain instructed Michael, "Lift the Mizzen sail on the stern so that we don't have to use the motor to run the boat along the trap line!" Taso knew that the warm calm breeze was nature's way of slowly moving the boat forward, and he wouldn't waste gasoline.

Michael quickly followed the Captain's orders, and the mizzen puffed to life, slowly moving the *Eagles Wing's* forward.

The Captain searched for the first signs of the trap line by finding its own unique buoy, a white oblong with light blue stripes and a white cross on its side, looking much like a Greek flag. "There she is," Taso exclaimed when seeing the first buoy bobbing on the surface like a harbor seals head.

Michael quickly moved to the starboard side where his father had already positioned himself ready to snag the first trap line with his gaff.

"Be careful Michael, I'm going to start the pot hauler now" Taso remarked as he reached into the wheelhouse to flip the switch that would send the pulley into motion, but also keeping an eye on where Michael was standing. "Yes Papa, I'm okay," Michael, commented, as the pulley came alive with its mechanical whirring sound. Michael then moved to the bait barrel, dragging it closer to where Taso was standing so that it would be in easy reach if the trap needed to be baited. The two fishermen were now ready to haul traps.

On many previous occasions, Michael, when watching his father effortlessly hoisting up traps, would ask, "Papa, can I try," and his father would always respond, "You are too young to do this, watch closely and learn... then someday you can try." But when Michael asked this day, Taso replied differently.

To Michael's surprise, his father paused for a moment, and then said, "Today is a special day for us... do you think you are ready to do this?" Michael's alert dark eyes opened wide and with a smile on his face, he blurted out with confidence, "Yes, of course I can!"

Taso was moved by the confidence expressed by his son, not to mention his new yellow pants and boots that made him look well prepared to take on the challenge. Whatever it was that made this moment different from the past, the Captain yielded to Michael's confidence and a turning point in their lives was about to begin.

"Okay Michael, let me take up the first trap while you watch carefully and I'll explain what's going on, then you can pull up the next trap." Michael nodded his head in assurance as he watched his father begin the first haul. Taso would work slowly, and exaggerate each detail so that Michael would learn first- hand, the art of Lobstering.

The Captain began by reaching for the long gaff pole, and

stretching it toward the buoy as he explained, "Make sure that you hook the gaff hook just below the buoy or else the buoy will slip off the gaff and we'll miss it and have to circle around for another try, and that's not good. We can lose a lot of precious time if that happens, and we have a lot of traps to haul today." Michael responded, "Yes Papa, I'll hook the gaff just under the buoy."

Then Taso continued by snagging the buoy and pulling it out of the water toward him, saying, "Now you've got to grab the buoy warp to put it onto the pot hauler's pulley, but I'll do that for you... at least until you can do it sometime later... got it?" "Yes Papa, you'll be putting the warp onto the pulley until when I can do it later," He repeated, making sure that his father knew that he understood the instruction.

Taso then carefully placed the warp onto the pulley, as he said, "Now watch carefully, the trap line is going to be pulled up quickly by the hauler, so watch as the toggle comes out first. The trap will come up right after the toggle. When the toggle jams into the pulley, the trap will be ready to grab and pull out of the water. It's going to be heavy, so hold onto it tightly and I'll help you pull it onto the rail, okay?"

Michael responded with confidence, "I'm strong Papa, I'll be able to hold onto it and pull it onto the rail." Taso paused before putting the warp onto the pulley, and repeated in a serious voice, "Now don't be so sure about how strong you are Michael, the traps are heavy, and you're probably going to need my help until you get used to moving these things around... do you understand?" "Yes Papa, I'll be careful" was his quick reply.

Taso carefully placed the warp onto the pulley as, all-hell-broke-loose, and the pulley grabbed the warp, sending water spraying outward and the warp flying across the deck. "Here comes the toggle, Michael," his father shouted, "now watch for the trap... here it comes." Almost magically the trap appeared at the surface as the toggle jammed into the pulley with a thud.

Taso instantly grabbed the trap and effortlessly lifted it

out of the water and onto the rail... water spilling in all directions from the trap's wooden slats. Michael looked on with amazement as his father's strong arms lifted the trap, making him wonder if he would be able do the same, in spite of his earlier words.

"Okay Michael, let's see what we have in the trap," as Taso slid the trap along the rail in one continuous motion and opened the trap's door.

Michael moved closer to the trap and looked on as his father probed inside for its hidden contents. "Let's see," he said as he first removed some muddied seaweed, a small crab and some clams. Then, one-after-another he pulled out three lobsters and measured them with his keepers gauge. Two of the three lobsters didn't make the cut and were thrown back into the water.

"Well Michael, it looks like we didn't do so good with this haul," as he placed the keeper into a basket behind him. "But maybe you'll do better on the next try. Now we'll have to put fresh bait into the trap and send it back till next time."

Michael was one step ahead of Taso and had already picked out some fresh bait from the bait barrel and placed it into the trap, without ever being asked to do so. Closing the trap door, Michael offered, "Is that okay?" Taso proudly answered, "Yes my son, now let's put it back in, but be careful as the warp drags across the deck when the trap falls overboard and into the water"

Taso removed the toggle from the davit and looked over to Michael to make sure that he was watching what he was about to do.

"Okay, here goes," he said as he pushed the trap off the rail and into the water. Immediately the trap sank, pulling the warp off the deck as it followed the trap. When the warp finally stopped following the trap, that was the signal that the trap had bottomed, and now to begin looking for another buoy farther along the line.

"Well my son, are you ready to try your luck?" Taso challenged Michael, as his memory once again shifted back to the time when he and his father had fished together for the first time. In an instant, Michael answered with confidence, "Yes Papa, I'm ready."

Taso looked on with pride and apprehension as he was re-living the time-honored tradition that now was being handed down to his own son

The proud father carefully guided the boat over to the next buoy, and in a short moment they were along-side of it. All the while, Taso was deeply focused on Michael, as he watched the boy move toward the rail where he would try his first attempt at Lobstering.

Normally, Tasos' seafaring instincts would be triggered by all the natural elements around him, like the feel of the wind, the smell of the air and the colors of the surrounding sky and water. However, Michael was occupying his mind now, and he was not paying much attention to the silently changing mood of the sea that was creeping over the boat.

Then, in a split second, a disturbing change in the mood of these elements sent a surprising and unexpected chill down his spine. Taso quickly glanced around to get his bearings on what the changes meant... but he couldn't see anything that made sense to him. The sky was bright blue and the mizzen sail was slack, indicating that there was no wind blowing.

In the meantime, Michael, standing at the same spot that his father had occupied just moments before was totally unaware of the change in the seas, and anxiously awaited the approaching buoy just ahead.

Suddenly, the waters took on a dark, ink-black iridescent color and began to churn as Taso struggled to hold the boat's position along-side the buoy. The temperature around the boat plummeted, sending a chill over the two fishermen, but mysteriously the sun continued to shine through a clear blue sky.

The Captain first thought that perhaps it was a shift in the wind that had triggered the sea's behavior, for the wind's direction was often known to change rapidly and without warning. But strangely, no wind could be felt on his face or seen on the mizzen sail, hanging limp from the short mast on the stern.

Taso had his hands full maneuvering the boat against the resistance of the seas, while instinctively looking for other signs to explain what was happening around the boat. He couldn't understand why the seas a short distance from the boat were calm and flat, but around the boat, the seas were turbulent. He sensed that something unusual was happening, and was about to tell Michael to hold off his attempt to bring up the next trap, when to his unexpected surprise Michael had already put into motion the next sequence of events.

In an instant, and without hesitation or directions from his father, Michael already had grabbed the gaff and thrust it out over the rail toward the buoy. Taso wouldn't have time to react to the beginning of the drama that was about to unfold.

To his father's surprise, Michael snatched the buoy perfectly. "Pull!" Taso instinctively shouted to Michael as he held tightly on the wheel. Michael responded quickly by pulling with all his strength. The gaff hook had securely looped around the buoy warp and then the buoy, but it wouldn't move upward into the boat. The trap, several fathoms below, was dragging along the bottom of the ocean, filling the trap with sand, rocks and any other object that got in its way.

The resistance of the trap seemed to be far greater than Michael's strength could handle, as the stern of the boat sank deeper into the water. "Careful now," the Captain said, "Grab the buoy and hand it to me, I'll try to break the trap loose with the pot hauler."

Taso knew that the next step was far too dangerous for Michael to do because the trap could suddenly break loose and knock Michael to the deck. Besides, even if the trap easily broke free, he would have to deal with the spinning pot hauler, which every seasoned fisherman had great fear and respect for.

Taso released his hold on the wheel and grabbed the warp, placing it over the pulley, and like before, water and warp went flying in every direction. The trap seemed to break loose from the bottom as the stern came up with a jolt, nearly knocking Michael off his feet.

Michael dropped the gaff and was concentrating on the warp being pulled from the water, awaiting the appearance of the toggle that would announce the impending trap. While this was happening, Taso went back to the pilothouse where he grabbed the wheel to try to keep the boat steady. Taso now realized that the temperature around the boat seemed to be at the point of freezing, as he observed ice crystals rapidly covering his gloves. Too many things were going on at the same time, and confusion clouded the Captain's mind as he tried to sort things out.

Then, the toggle came flying out of the water and jammed into the pot hauler, indicating that the trap was in position to be grabbed.

Taso shouted to Michael, "Leave it alone," as he knew that he had to get control of the boat before dragging the trap into it, but again he was too late, for Michael had already reached over the rail with both hands and grabbed the trap. At the very same time, the boat shifted violently upward as if a wave had overtaken it. Taso's left hand had instantly frozen onto the Ship's wheel, with black ice completely encapsulating his gloved hand.

Although Taso tried desperately to free his hand from the wheel, the freezing ink-black waters that had surrounded the boat, were also holding him captive to it. He apprehensively looked back toward Michael, who now was struggling to pull the trap out of the water. "Let go of the trap!" he shouted to Michael, fearing that he too would have his hands frozen to it. But Michael was not able to let go of it for a different reason. Something below the water seemed to have power over Michael's hands as he tried to let go but couldn't.

"Papa, I can't... it won't let go of me!" Michael was strong for a twelve year old, but the trap would test his strength as never before.

Michael's determination was not about to give in to the struggle, and Taso was in no position to come to his son's aide. With all his strength, Michael tugged upward but nothing seemed to happen as if some unknown force were tugging back and trying to pull Michael into the water. As the boat rocked port-to-starboard, water began to come in over the rail and onto the deck, threatening to swamp the boat.

With his free hand, Taso reached for the bilge pump switch and flipped it upward to turn it on so that the water would be pumped out of the boat... but nothing happened. Without the bilge pump, the boat could not handle any more water coming in. Now both the boat and the two fishermen's lives were in serious trouble.

With an effort summoned from deep within his body, Michael pulled as hard as he could to lift the trap out of the water and into the boat. The force behind the trap began to release its grip and the trap moved upward about halfway onto the rail as water gushed out of it in every direction. For just a moment, the Captain felt a sigh of relief, seeing the trap move toward the rail where Michael might possibly get control of it.

Then to his and Michael's surprise, the cold water gushing from the trap spilled over the rail and into Michaels yellow oilskins, making him lose his balance and fall to his knees... but never releasing his grip on the trap. Taso felt helpless as he watched his son being overtaken by a force that even he couldn't understand, as his frozen hand was held even tighter to the wheel.

Michael was unable to let go of the trap as the strange force behind it began to retreat into the cold waters below, dragging Michael up on his feet and half over the outside rail. Taso watched helplessly as the force began to overtake Michael.

The blur of time seemed to move into slow motion as the tug-of-war continued. Taso's heart beat faster as he tried to release his hand, pounding on the black ice that encapsulated it with his free hand, but with no relief. He then frantically stretched back toward Michael with his free hand to try to keep the child from being taken overboard. But as hard as he tried, he couldn't break his fingers loose to reach his son. The helpless Taso now feared that Michael would soon be taken into the hungry belly of the sea, and he could only watch it happen.

Despair overcame Taso as tears filled his eyes, blurring his vision. "No... no!" he cried, "You can't take him away from us!" Taso was now speaking to the evil force that was trying to hurt Michael.

Then from deep within Taso's soul, he could hear a soft, calm voice speak to him, "Reach for the bell... the sounds of man and nature shall never be silenced." Instantly he recalled the time when he and Alexandra had experienced the same danger on their first trip together, and the locket being torn from her neck. His mind could hear the sound of the bell that ended the danger. Then he flashed to the image of Shawn, lying injured on his boat, saying, "At the sound of the bell, the pulley let me free."

Not knowing what else to do, Taso yelled out, "Hold on Michael... don't let go... we're coming!" Taso didn't know why he said; "We're coming," for only he and Michael were on the boat. Then, his free hand seemed to be guided toward the ship's bell, where its clapper rope laid waiting.

Michael's body was about to be dragged overboard when Taso's hand finally reached the rope, and he pulled it sharply downward. The bell came alive with a loud pealing sound that resonated across the water in an endless echo that seemed to go on forever. At that same instant, his frozen glove-hand melted free from the wheel, and he lunged for Michael... grabbing him by the back of his oil skin pants, keeping him inside the boat.

With one hand on Michael's pants and the other now grabbing hold of the bulkhead, the Captain held on tightly. Michael concentrated on the trap, never releasing his grip and pulled with all his might.

Then, to both Michael's and the Captain's surprise, the battle ended almost as quickly as it had begun.

The force behind the trap stopped pulling at Michael, and the trap seemed to become weightless as Michael easily gained control over it.

Then, as if the trap was being lifted out of the water by unseen helping hands, it rose to the rail and was gently laid in front of Michael. The seas beyond the rail stopped churning and changed back to a pale blue color as the warm sun spread its rays over the exhausted men. With eyes wide open and adrenalin streaming through his veins, Taso whispered the words, "Thank you God... thank you Alex!"

During the brief silence that followed the terror-filled moments, the only sound that could be heard, was that of the two fishermen gasping for air to fill their oxygen-depleted lungs, and the whirring sound of the bilge pump that was now working effortlessly clearing water from inside the boat.

Taso's muscles burned as if fire were streaming through his veins, causing his arms to tremble as he tried to gather his strength to embrace his son. But before he could do so, the silence was shattered by Michael's excited voice as it echoed out, "I did it... I did it!" And his giant eyes and mother's smile gazed upon the treasure retrieved from the sea.

Taso was frozen with pride, but dizzied by the confusion of what had just happened, as he watched his son dance in circles on the deck of the boat, water draining out from the bottoms of his shiny yellow pants. Taso was seeing himself in his son's movements, just as he had danced in circles around the baby Michael so many times before on the floor of their house.

Not wanting to end the celebration, the proud father offered, "Not so fast my son, you're not done yet, you must now finish the job."

Michael was so excited that he was barely able to continue. He rushed back to the trap and searched for the latch to begin his inspection of its hidden treasures, the same inquisitive way that he examined the creatures found at the shore.

Slowly reaching in, he grabbed some dripping wet seaweed and tossed it into the water. Next he found a sea urchin, and asked, "What should I do with him, Papa?" The Captain's mind momentarily drifted back to a day long ago when Alexandra watched as an urchin was snagged by a gull, and a lesson in life was learned.

Instinctively Taso glanced upward, almost expecting to see a gull, ready to swoop down, but none were in sight. "Release him back into the sea where he can live in harmony with nature." Michael gently placed the urchin over the rail close to the water and opened his hand, allowing it to roll off into the water.

Next, Michael reached back into the trap and found a small wriggling crab and carefully examined it to see if it had been injured. "It's all right Papa," and he carefully released it back into the sea, just as he had done with those creatures nursed back to health from the fish boxes back home.

Once again he reached into the trap, and one-after-another pulled out six very large lobsters... all of which were keepers.

Taso was astounded as he gazed at the bounty retrieved by his son, placing them in the basket behind him.

"No wonder the trap was so heavy," he said." I would have had trouble pulling it in myself, and you did it all by yourself!" again pausing to think of how not just Michael and he alone were in the struggle, but also an unseen guiding hand.

When all the living creatures in the trap had been removed, Michael looked back into it where sand; mud and rocks were gathered on its bottom. Michael asked, "Papa, what should we do with all this stuff?" Taso looked in and said, "You'll have to clean it out and re-bait the trap."

Michael reached in and began to remove the debris. He tossed a few large rocks out and then began sifting through the mud-like sand. His small hands could only handle a little at a time, as he slowly proceeded to empty the trap. When he finally came to the last few handfuls, something shiny peeked from below the wet sand.

Michael probed deeper into it with his fingers, un-burying a strange shiny object. Finally, Michael's hand cleared the remaining sand and a heart-shaped locket was left clinging to the bottom of the trap.

"What is it Papa," Michael asked as Taso looked on with disbelief. "It can't be!" Taso exclaimed, as he lifted the locket from the bottom of the trap. "It can't be!" He shouted even louder as he brought the locket closer to his eyes.

"What is it Papa?" Michael once again asked, as his father slowly grabbed the two sides of the locket and opened it, revealing a fragment of washed out paper on the right side, and an image of Michael the Archangel on the left side.

"It's a miracle Michael, that's what it is… it's a miracle!" Taso shouted as his hands closed upon the locket and he fell to his knees. His head slowly bent low, as he cupped his hands over his face and began to weep… his body trembling as twelve years of built-up tears were spilled out onto the deck.

He could feel the loneliness and grief that had imprisoned him for so long a time, slowly being released by the presence of Alexandra's spirit, in the locket that he held tightly within his hands.

Michael had never seen his father cry before, and instinctively moved close to him, placing his arms around his shoulders and then burying his head onto his shoulder. Michael wasn't sure about what had just happened, and began to think that he was the reason for all of the chaos that had transpired. "Papa, I'm sorry for what happened, I didn't know it was going be so hard… I should have waited before I tried to lift the trap," he offered as he buried his head deeper into his father's shoulder.

Taso was drained with emotion as he pulled Michael close to him and hugged him, saying, "No... no my son, you didn't do anything wrong. You did everything perfectly, I'm so proud of you. I don't understand what happened myself, but for sure, we're a family today... and your mother is with us, and she also brought a friend to help."

Michael was more confused than ever with Taso's words, but it didn't matter to him, for he was in his father's strong arms and felt more secure than he had ever felt in his life. Then turning his attention back to the locket, he inquired, "Papa, what's that shiny thing that was in the bottom of the trap?"

Taso opened his hand and showed the locket to Michael, tears still clouding his eyes, saying, "Michael, this is a locket that I gave to your mother the very first time that she and I were on the boat together. We came to this same place, where I gave it to her as a gift of love and protection before we were married. The locket had my picture on one side, but you see, it's gone. On the other side is Michael the Archangel." Taso turned the locket toward Michael and showed him the image of the angel that he just spoke of.

"You were named after Michael the Archangel, who was chosen by God to be the protector of man when we are in difficult times. Anyway, something happened that day, and the locket got snagged on a trap as it was being returned to the water. That's when it fell overboard and sank before we could grab it. Your mother was very saddened about losing it, and we were sure that it was gone forever. But here we are today, at the very same spot where the locket was lost, and we also were in trouble. I'm still not sure what happened while struggling with the trap, but we were protected through it all. Somehow I was drawn to the ship's bell by a silent voice that sounded like your mother's. When the bell released its sound, it seemed to call to the angel, and the danger ended... I just don't know. I'm sure that somehow when the trap was dragged along the bottom, it must have scooped-up the locket where it laid there waiting for you to get it back. And here it is again, after all these years... it's a miracle!"

Michael then asked, "Did the angel help us today... and is that the friend you were talking about?" Taso just smiled as he nodded in agreement, turning his head toward the ship's bell and said, "Yes my son, he is the friend that we have with us all the time, especially when we need him most."

Taso rose, and taking Michael by the hand, went to the brass trimmed storage box that held two linen napkins... he opened it and removed one of the napkins. The locket was carefully placed inside the napkin, and then carefully folded and returned to the box where it awaited its safe return home along with the fishermen.

Taso and Michael had now become "the Captain and his Mate," as they went on to fish the waters along the shoal. Cautiously, they proceeded along the trap line to retrieve a third trap. Taso reached for the trap, as the gaff did its work and drew the buoy into the boat. Each trap thereafter came up, unhindered by weather or any other unforeseen surprises.

Working side-by-side, the two fishermen proceeded as if they had been doing this forever, as they retrieved a bounty of gifts from the sea. It would have been impossible to determine who was having more fun or who had more pride as the day drew on. Taso' heart once again felt a strange peace that had long been forgotten as he, Michael, and the spirit of Alexandra were together on the boat.

Time flew by and before they knew it, the end of the trap line was in site. As they pulled the last trap into the boat and opened it expecting to find an abundance of lobsters, just as the previous traps yielded, they were shocked to find absolutely nothing... not even dead seaweed and mud.

Taso reached over to Michael, placed his hands on his shoulders, and looking into his eyes he spoke in a deliberate and serious tone, "See, my son, God is reminding us not to be so greedy, and that we should be patient with the gifts given to us. Let's go home to rest and thank God for all the special gifts that He's given to us today."

In Taso's heart, he knew that the day had been one of profound enlightenment, and that the painful burden of loneliness held for so long had been removed. For the first time since the day Alexandra spoke her final words to him and the defenseless newborn Michael being held in his arms, peace had finally come to him. In Taso' mind, he could still hear her words, "Love him and guide him... teach him that God's peace replaces all fear." This day, her words were lived out on that small colorful fishing boat.

The physical and emotionally drained fishermen were ready to end their day, as Taso steered the boat back toward the Cove and opened the throttle... the motor responding in agreement with its recognizable, putt-putting sound.

Taso then called to Michael, "Come here at my side and help me guide the boat home!" Michael smiled with pride, taking a position at his father's side as the warm sun reflected off the calm, pale-blue waters of the cove.

The Captain reached for Michael's hands and placed them on the wheel, saying... "Take us home son!" Then he stepped behind the young fisherman and reached once more for the bell rope, snapping it downward, releasing a sound that peeled outward in a never-ending echo announcing a newfound peace and harmony between man and nature.

Chapter Fourteen

When the day ended for the fishermen, they returned to the wharf with their abundant catch and proud story of how Michael had fished along-side his father. The boat was cleaned and prepped for the next day and they loaded their truck with the goods taken from the sea, to be sold at the commercial seafood buyer's terminal. The money traded for the catch that day would be generous... and for a long time thereafter, peace would settle upon the Pappas family.

On the way home, Taso and Michael stopped at Shawn's repair shop to drop off some of the lobsters and clams that had been reaped from the harvest that day. When they arrived, Shawn was working on a winch motor as the fishermen entered the open doors to the shop.

Shawn glanced up and an immediate smile emerged upon his face as he reached for a red shop cloth hanging out of his back trouser pocket. He wiped his hands clean as he briskly walked toward Taso and Michael. Shawn then proclaimed with a broad smile on his face as if royalty had entered his domain, "Welcome my friends!" and shook Taso's hand. Then he followed, by placing his other hand on Michael's head saying, "Yup my boy, you're sure growing up quickly, why it seemed that you could hardly climb up over the rail of your daddy's boat not so long ago... but look at you now! Soon you'll be as big as your daddy and able to help him haul those lobsters." Taso quickly interrupted Shawn and offered, "Not soon Shawn, but now... today."

Shawn turned to Taso whose proud grin preceded his next statement. "My boy has become a man today and pulled traps along my side, working every bit as hard as I did. We had a little trouble on the boat... but we made it through it together. Something strange happened around the boat, as the seas turned wild, and we started to take on water. While all this was happening, one of our traps dragged along the bottom, and Michael held on till it released. When we finally got it into the boat, we cleared the trap and look what we found," Taso reached into his pocket and removed the linen napkin that held the locket. Carefully opening it he showed it to Shawn. "What is that?" Shawn asked. "It's the locket that I gave to Alexandra when we were first engaged."

Shawn was astounded, as he remembered the story about the locket when he and Megan were at the hospital after Alexandra became ill when Michael was born. "You've got to be kidding!" he offered, as he stared at the locket.

Just then, Megan came through the door that separated the shop from their home and went straight to Michael, giving him a hug as she always did.

"Hi guys!" She exclaimed as she then approached Taso to give him an equally welcoming hug. Shawn quickly interrupted the welcoming embraces as he repeated Taso's story about the resurrected locket.

Megan gasped at seeing the locket as she put her hands over her mouth in disbelief. "I can't believe it!" she sighed, as the locket dangled from Taso's hand. Megan had remembered the story of the lost locket when Alexandra had shared it with her years ago, and tears began to stream from her eyes. Taso then tried to explain the depth of what had occurred.

"Today a miracle happened to Michael and me, and I'm sure that Alexandra was part of it all. When the locket was lost that day, a long time ago, I tried to console Alexandra, saying that the locket was only a symbol of our love... and that a mere symbol couldn't separate our love for one another. But I was wrong, because since that moment when we watched the locket sink into the dark waters below the boat... I watched

Alexandra's heart sink along with it. I now realize that love is so powerful, that any gift given out of love has great power. And when we receive a gift out of love... even a symbolic one, it becomes a part of who we are."

"Finding the locket, after it was seemingly lost and gone forever, symbolizes our eternal life as family. The locket had to be retrieved so that it would always be a constant reminder of the power of love. We weren't in this alone; we had help from our friend, Michael the Archangel."

"I'm not sure what force was trying to destroy the power of our love, but our faith was more powerful than it was... and we overcame the struggle."

The depth of what Taso was saying was much deeper than what Michael and the Fosters could ever comprehend, but they too knew that something special had happened that day... and the locket was testimony to it. The gift of the locket would become a constant reminder and confirmation... that God's love transcends all fear.

Shawn and Megan felt the same peace that Taso and Michael had shared with them, and more loving embraces were exchanged as the two fishermen had to part from their good friends. As always, Megan paused her goodbye, as she retreated back into her kitchen to snatch some freshly baked treats for the fishermen.

When she returned, her arms held a brown paper bag full of hot bread and cookies, which she proudly handed to Taso, exclaiming; "Now you enjoy this with your meal tonight!" And looking toward Michael, she said, "You might just find a few chocolate chip cookies somewhere in the bag." Michael smiled back at Megan, and then ran toward her with his arms wide open, and gave her a slow hug, saying, "Thank you for the cookies, I'll save one for Papa!" And they all laughed at Michael's response.

Michael and Taso then returned to the truck for the ride home, but before Taso could start the engine, Michael said to his father, "Mr. Foster sure is nice, and Mrs. Foster makes good cookies, doesn't she?" Michael was familiar with Megan's baked goods, for he had enjoyed them on many previous occasions.

"Yes," said Taso, "we are fortunate to have friends like the Fosters, and they're good people who care for one another and many other people in Black Point Cove. Megan... I mean Mrs. Foster, loves you as if you were her child, and she would do anything for you. She was your mama's best friend, and when she and Mr. Foster became your godparents at baptism, they vowed to love and protect you if anything would happen to me. You are a very lucky child to have so many people love you the way they do!"

The familiar chain of questions from Michael continued, as he asked, "Papa... what was my Mama like... did she know me?" At this, Taso became silent as tears filled his eyes and his mind instantly flashed to clouded images of Alexandra. He could see her magical smile and feel her body pressed against his, just as it did when she announced the impending birth of Michael. Then he recalled those last images of her weakened, but smiling face when she caressed Michael and uttered her last words, "I give you this son out of my deepest love for you ... love him and guide him... teach him that God's peace replaces fear."

For a moment, Taso had been lost in this lingering memory, when Michael's voice broke the trance... "Papa, are you okay?" At this, Taso directed his attention back to Michael. "Yes Michael, I'm okay, and we are blessed to have had your mother as part of our lives."

"Your mother knew very much who you were... well before you were born, and she loved you with a love that united your spirit with hers. Her very last gesture before she died was to caress your small body and give you her love. She promised us that her love for us would last forever, and she kept her promise today on the boat."

"Michael, you are a very special child, filled with the love and spirit that your mother had. She will be your guiding light and will always be a part of who you are."

"Whenever I look at you, I see her. You have her smile, which shows her beauty and love for life. My son, I love you also, and with God's help we both are guided by her spirit of love for us... just like the lighthouse guides us when we are lost. Mama loved you with the deepest love a person could give, and if she were here with us now, she would have her arm around you, and would be reminding us that when God enters our life, fear is replaced by peace."

Then Taso removed the gold locket from his shirt pocket, glanced at it with loving admiration, and then handed it to Michael, saying, "The locket, which is more than a symbol of love, is now yours... keep it with you always, and remember that the angel is only a thought away. Today my son, we lived your mother's words. When we were in trouble on the boat, we saw how the guiding hand of God replaced my fear when you had your hands full, fighting with the trap. Your mother's words have certainly become a part of who we are, and we will always need them in our life's journey."

At that, Michael smiled back at his father, "Papa, I think that I love Mama too, because I almost never feel lost... so she must be guiding me too."

Taso knew that enough had been said. "Well my son, we have both felt the peace that love brings to us, let's go home."

The days and weeks following the fishermen's liberation from fear were filled with peace and harmony as Taso and Michael continued fishing the ledge where the mysterious ordeal had taken place. And while school would be starting in a few short weeks for Michael, the remaining summer days would be cherished as they spent the time in each other's company.

Each day that summer, their catch was larger than any previous year, and they became the envy of all of the other fishermen in the cove. And at the end of each day, Taso watched as Michael, proudly wearing his yellow oilskins would clean and polish the bell that somehow had intervened in their lives.

The bell had become a symbol of hope and peace to Taso

and Michael, if only to focus them on the undying love of Alexandra... or perhaps the Archangel Michael, whose promise of protection was always with them.

Nonetheless, their respect for the bell became a secret part of their lives, and they would always honor its presence.

During the time that Taso and Michael were enjoying each other's company, and successfully gathering an abundance of lobsters from the ledge, something different was happening to the other fishermen in the Cove. Each day, the other fishermen's catches were dwindling, and the Black Point Cove Co-op was not as successful as once it had been. Only Taso was catching enough lobsters... and a lot more at that.

The other fishermen were beginning to feel that Taso's assigned area along the ledge had given him an advantage over them. This situation created some resentment that the *Eagles Wing's* was somehow better than the other fishing boat's. When Taso and Michael would come back to the docks at the end of the day, they were no longer greeted with smiles and handshakes... but strained looks.

Taso was well aware of the situation, and couldn't explain why his area was doing so much better than the others. But on the upcoming Thursday, a meeting of the Co-op's partners would begin to reveal what might be the cause.

When the Thursday evening Black Point Co-op meeting finally came, everyone assembled in the church's gathering hall to discuss the problem. And as usual, sitting in the back of the room was Crock, waiting to share his wisdom of the sea. But tonight, he would not be the one focused upon.

Taso and Michael were the last to arrive at the gathering hall where the Co-op typically would meet. A hush came over the assembly as Taso directed Michael to a chair next to Crock in the back of the room. Then he proceeded to the front of the room with the other Co-op leaders, where he took the last vacant seat at the head table. All eyes silently stared toward the head table... the meeting was about to begin... as a gavel sent its alarming call to order.

As usual, Father Benning was present, and opened the meeting with a prayer for all the fishermen. Then, the finance officer read the state of affairs. The news was not good, net income was down to a level never before seen. When the finance report indicated that Taso had the highest percentage gain in the whole Co-op, a wave of groans and murmurs echoed across the hall.

Ned Burrows was the first to speak out, "For the last three months, I've lost my pants trying to fish for lobsters, and my traps aren't getting any hit's at all. I can hardly pay my bait bill, and gas and oil for my boat are killing me. It seems as though something has scared all the fish away from the Cove. I'm not the only one having trouble, you're all in the same boat as I am." Then looking over to Taso, Ned continued on, "Except Pappas over there!" as he pointed a finger in the Captain's direction. "He's got a great spot along the ledge, and is pulling up more of them critters as I've ever seen before... what are we doing wrong, and what's he doing right?"

The murmuring continued louder, as confusion took over the meeting. Then from the back of the room, Crock yelled out in an agitated tone, "Hold on a minute you scallywags, Captain Pappas is a good man and yuz all know that he's a bin sharing everything he's ever had with ya all. So quit yer bellyaching and get down to what the problems really are... don't go a blaimin summon far nothin he has ta do with!"

The murmurs silenced as everyone began to realize that the problem wasn't with Taso... but they still had no knowledge of what was keeping the lobsters out of their traps.

Taso hadn't said a word until now, but then he spoke in a calm, compassionate voice, "Folks, I can see that you're all having a tough time fishing, and maybe I can help. I've been blessed with our catch, and will be willing to share it with all of you. It wouldn't be right for Michael and I not to share what God has allowed us to take from the Cove. So, I've decided to split up all of my catch equally among you until we figure out what we can do to make things better.

The crowd went silent, as Taso's unselfish offer couldn't

be disputed. Ned answered for the whole Co-op when he responded to Taso's offer, "Captain Pappas, I'm sorry for speaking the way I did a moment ago, but I guess that my pride just got in the way of my brain. Crock's right, you've been a friend of the cove for a long time, and your Mom and Dad before you. You're a good man for all you've done, and we can't help but thank you again for your offer."

Taso wasn't about to let his own pride get in the way with what really needed to be done... and that was to figure out what was happening in the deep waters of the cove. Taso's words of assurance followed, "What we need to do is to figure out what's happening in the cove... anyone have anything to offer that might give us a clue?"

The crowd began to murmur among themselves again, and finally a hand rose from within the middle of the group.

It was Tom Moody, a long-time resident and well-respected fisherman. "Hey folks, I don't know if this has anything to do with the problem, but I seem to think that the problem might be related to the water." The crowd buzzed with agreement as Tom continued, "I've noticed that the water west of the cove seems to be murky, and darker than I've ever seen it before. Yes, from time to time I've see it turn dark black, but it cleaned up real quick and everything was okay after that. Now, it seems to be constantly black, and I swear, the iridescent color scares me, and the fish don't seem to like it either." The crowd agreed, as they one by one offered similar comments about the strange colored water.

Taso then chimed in, "Seems to be a consensus here, something's wrong with the water. I've heard of the "Red Blight" before... you know, when the water gets real red and the shellfish die out. But that's not what Tom's describing... seems to be something else. My suggestion is for us to get some expert help from the Maine Oceanography Sciences in Portland. Perhaps someone there can pinpoint the problem. I'd be glad to contact them and see if someone can come up to the Cove and nose around a bit."

The crowd was in agreement, as indicated by nodding heads

and murmurs. Ned then seemed to speak for the group, offering his comments as if to end the meeting, "Thanks Pappas, we'd be grateful if you'd make the contact, and we'll try to figure this thing out. And by the way, we really thank you for your offer, and hope we can return the favor someday."

Nothing more needed to be said, as Father Benning rose to offer a closing prayer... making the sign of the cross and beginning; "Father, we know of your generosity and blessings upon this community, and trust that your promise of peace and hope will become our path to righteousness... Amen!"

The men of the Co-op stood up silently, and one by one, each shaking Taso's hand, whispered their personal thanks as they left.

After everyone was gone, from the back of the room, Michael ran toward his father, followed by Crock, hobbling behind. "Papa, what do you think is in the water that's making the fish scarred?"

Taso looked at Michael and answered in a manner that hinted that he might be on to something, "I'm not sure Michael, but we'll figure this thing out?" Crock just looked on and knew that if anyone could solve the problem, Taso might just be the one.

Chapter Fifteen

The last days of August were waning when the morning sun was still below the horizon in anticipation of a new day. Michael wasn't ready to wake, as he lay on his side, motionless beneath a cotton sheet pulled up to his ears. Looking down at the sleeping child, Taso felt his love swell, and thought of how truly blessed he was to have Michael as a part of his life. But something was chewing at Taso's mind, and he would have to wake Michael to join him in its unraveling.

"Michael!" the Captain whispered, as the child's deep sleep kept out the invitation to rise, "Michael" he said again as he softly placed his hand on Michael's shoulder, gently moving it so as not to startle him. The shadowy frame of Michael slowly moved as if adjusting his posture to a more comfortable position. Once again Taso whispered, "Michael, you must get up now, we have something very important to do!"

Slowly Michael turned onto his back and opened his eyes to see his father looking down on him. Michael's first reaction was to smile at his father, but was immediately followed by a confused reaction. "Papa, what is it?" Taso whispered back to Michael, "Get up son, we are about to go fishing for a problem!" Michael had learned a long time ago to trust his father without asking too many questions, and this time was no different than before.

Michael quickly rose from the bed and headed toward the bathroom, when Taso interrupted his path, "Michael, do what you need to do, but don't linger too much, someone is waiting for us... so be quick!" The sleepy Michael responded, still half asleep, "Yes Papa, I'll hurry."

Taso turned to leave the room and headed toward the kitchen where his guest was sitting with his hands wrapped around a cup of steaming coffee.

"Well Tom... Michael will be down in a minute, and then we can go." Sitting across the table was Tom Moody, who had offered his comments at the Co-op meeting a week before. At the meeting, Taso's heart seemed to flutter as Tom described the water just like he had experienced several times before... once with Alexandra, again when Shawn had his mishap, and once more with Michael, before the fishing seemed to go bad. Taso wanted to know more, and a trip out toward the west end of the Cove just might provide some clue as to what was happening.

"Tom, I appreciate you taking us out to look at that murky water you were describing during the meeting. Before I contact the Oceanography Science people in Portland, I want to see what you're talking about so that I can explain the situation more clearly to them."

Tom took a long sip from the cup, placed it back on the table, and answered, "Yep Pappas, I didn't like the look of the water out there. It just seemed to go bad in front of my eyes. Some fish just floated up on the surface... dead. Then, none of my traps had any live lobsters in them; they too were dead... every one of them. I've never seen anything like it before, that's why I mentioned it." Then looking over to Taso as he once again picked up the coffee and drew a long sip, he stopped and said, "What do you think it is?" Taso answered as if he hadn't a clue what it might be, but down deep inside, he felt differently, "I don't know, Tom, but maybe we'll know more this morning."

Just then, Michael entered the kitchen and looked up at Tom who was sitting at the table. "Good morning Mister Moody," Michael said in a surprised voice, then turning toward his father, a look of confusion covered his face. Taso reacted quickly, "Okay Michael, here's a cup of hot chocolate and a piece of cake that Megan sent over. Just take it with us as we go over to Tom's boat for a ride."

"Yes Papa" was his reply as he reached for the cup, took a quick sip and grabbed the cake. "Let's go Tom, we won't have much time before the sun comes up and spoils our investigation."

The trip out to the western waters of the Cove didn't take long, as Tom's boat, much faster than the *Eagles Wing's* quickly carried the three fishermen to its destination. Soon, the motor slowed to a crawl as Tom looked over the rail for whatever had triggered his concern. It was still very dark out, but eager eyes scanned the surface for clues to the mystery. No one spoke, as they continued to scan the waters. Then, Tom's voice shrieked out, startling Michael and Taso, "There it is... I see it, look over there!" as Tom pointed off the port side of the boat.

Taso and Michael moved to the port side where Tom was looking right over the rail along-side of the boat. "See that," he said, pointing down toward the water.

All eyes were focused on the water along-side the boat, and sure enough, the water seemed to look different from what they would normally see.

While the water was certainly darker than normal, it also seemed to be thick, as if it were syrup. Looking closer, they noticed a strange menacing glow, not bright, but more of a deep purple iridescent ultra-violet sort of color. "See that!" Tom exclaimed as his finger continued to point over the rail. "Yes Tom, I see," came the reply from Taso's lips as he and Michael stared at the glowing darkness.

"What do you think it is Pappas?" Tom questioned as if he expected Taso to know exactly what it was, but Taso just kept saying, "I just don't know... this is where the ledge drops off pretty steeply. I'm not sure how deep it is here or what's below the water. This is the place where a deep crevice was discovered many years ago, but the depth couldn't be determined because it was deeper than anyone could measure. No one knows for sure what might exist within the crevice, nor what might be coming out of it due to shifts in the geological structure of the land below us, you know... maybe a tectonic plate shift or earthquake or something similar"

For the next half hour or so, Taso and Tom maneuvered the boat into several different positions within the mass of strange colored water. Every so often a dead fish would float past the observers and send a sobering chill over them... or was it a different sort of chill that surrounded the boat?

Finally, the morning sun broke the horizon, making it difficult to see the subtle glowing mass surrounding the boat. Taso eventually broke the silent investigation by offering, "Well Tom, I think I've seen enough, and will be able to describe it to the people in Portland. Hopefully someone there is smarter than we are, and can unravel what it is, and if it's what's causing the problem. Let's get back to the harbor, and I'll get a call placed to Portland right away!"

Tom obliged Taso, and was happy to leave the murky glowing water. His motor groaned louder as it lunged forward, and in a half hour they were approaching the dock where the other fishermen were just leaving for the day. Tom, Taso and Michael were met with strange curious looks as the other boat's streamed past them leaving the harbor, but no fish or lobsters would be caught today.

When Tom's boat arrived at the dock, Taso thanked him for his help in seeing what he had described at the meeting. "Thanks Tom, I'll be sure to tell the folks in Portland about the water we saw earlier, hopefully they'll be able to help... have a good day!"

Taso guided Michael off the dock and decided to take the path along the shore that led back home. When they reached the familiar stone bench below their house, Taso stopped and sat down, and Michael followed his lead by sitting next to his father.

During all that happened that morning, Michael had not spoken a word, but was taking in all that his father had said.

Finally he broke his silence and said to his father, "Papa, you're on to something, but I don't know what it is. I saw in your eyes that you were looking deeper into the water than mister Moody was. Did you see something that we couldn't?"

Taso turned to Michael, and spoke quietly, as if he didn't want anyone to hear what he was about to say. "Michael, I didn't see anything that you or Mr. Moody didn't see, but I did have a feeling deep inside of me that sent a chill down my back."

"I felt the same way that I felt several times before, just like I did when we were on our boat fighting that trap. Whatever was fighting us then, is what is fighting us now. The only difference is that it moved away from Praying Rock, and settled in the western part of the cove, just before Black Rock Cliff." I don't think the people in Portland will know what it is, but I have a feeling that I do... but I'm not sure what to do about it."

Michael, in a quizzing voice, as if he was challenging his father to spew out the obvious answer, said, "Well Papa, just do what you did then, and maybe it'll go away."

For a moment, Taso continued to stare out to sea, as if the challenge went unheard. Then as if an explosion of understanding came forth from his brain, Taso jumped to his feet and turned to Michael, grabbed his shoulders and shouted, "That's it... the bell!"

Michael was startled at his father's reaction, and just stood there in awe saying, "Papa, what are you talking about... the bell." Taso immediately stopped talking and carefully looked around to see if anyone was around. Then he turned back to Michael and said, "Tomorrow morning we'll see who the culprit is, and maybe, just maybe we'll send it on a long vacation." Michael looked on in confusion, but once again he knew that his father was up to something, and as before, trust was all that was needed to satisfy his concern.

****

The next morning Taso got up early, and proceeded to Michael's room to wake him, assured that he would be sound asleep, since it was well before dawn.

When Taso quietly opened the door, he was surprised to see Michael already dressed, and sitting patiently at the foot of his bed. "Good morning Papa, I'm ready to go!" Michael said with a smile on his face. "Good morning Michael, I see that you're anxious to go fishing today," Michael just smiled back as he rose to his feet and gave his father a hug, saying, "I am anxious... do you think we'll catch anything?" Taso just looked back and said, "Only if we're lucky." Then they left for the short trip to the dock.

When they reached the dock, the *Eagles Wing's* could be seen bobbing carelessly, awaiting their arrival. Taso disregarded the ritual of putting on his oilskins and boots, and went right to the pilothouse and started the motor. Without hesitation the motor came alive as if it too were anxious to begin the day's adventure.

The mooring ropes were removed from their cleats, and the boat putt-putted away from the dock toward the west. Neither Taso nor Michael spoke a word as the boat journeyed toward Black Rock Cliff. When they arrived, about twenty minutes later, the motor was stopped, and Taso tossed the boat's anchor overboard, although it would never touch the deep bottom. "This is that place where the depth of the drop off could not be measured, so this just might be the place to start our fishing. Well Michael," Taso quietly whispered, as if someone could hear his words, "Are you ready to fish?" Although Michael was sure that they weren't going to fish, his confident response was, "Yes I am, but what do you want me to do?"

Taso answered, "I'm not sure, but stay close to me and we'll figure this out together." Then Taso went over to the ornately trimmed box where Alexandra's and his parent's napkins were stored. He opened the box and removed the napkins, giving Alexandra's to Michael, while he kept his father's napkin. "Put the napkin into your pocket, and I'll do the same with mine." Michael followed his father's instructions, without question. Then Taso reached once again into the box and removed a small wrench and white polishing cloth from it. "While I work on the bell, you look over the side rail to try and find that black glowing water again."

Michael was more confused than ever, but followed his father's instructions, and quickly moved to the rail to look for the strange water.

Taso moved toward the bell, but Michael couldn't see what he was doing because his father was standing between him and the bell. Nonetheless, Michael scanned the water in hopes of seeing the strange water.

Then, there it was, right below the rail of the boat. Michael's excitement broke the silence as he shouted, "Papa, it's here, right along-side of the boat... what should I do?"

Taso turned immediately and moved along side of Michael to see what he had discovered. "Yes" Taso said sarcastically, as if he were greeting an enemy. "We meet once again."

Michael looked on, as he was seeing something in his father's eyes that he had never seen before. Taso had somehow taken control of the eerie situation and was speaking to the water as if it were alive.

"What are we going to do now, Papa?" Michael asked, as his father stared into the iridescent glowing mass below the boat.

"We must put our trust in things that are sometimes not seen," was his reply. Then Taso turned back toward the bell where he had almost finished removing the clevis pin, which held the bell onto its pivot frame. Then, as if by magic, the bell emerged in Taso's hands, shining more brightly than it had ever shined before. As he carried the bell toward the rail, the fragrant smell of sea roses seemed to settle over the boat.

Beyond the rail, the cold black waters began to bubble like boiling thick syrup. Taso reached the rail where Michael was watching as the mood around the boat was changing, at first just subtly but then more rapidly. Taso looked directly at

Michael and spoke to him in a careful and deliberate way.

"Michael, I want you to do something that will help us destroy the black water. You alone have a gift, and this bell is part of it. I want you to take the bell in your hands, and touch the water with it... can you do that?" Michael looked back at his father, and answered without hesitation, "Yes, I can!"

Taso then instructed Michael to remove the linen napkin from his pocket and wrap it around the ringed loop at the top of the bell, to keep it from sliding out of his hands. Michael followed the instructions, and soon the ringed loop at the top of the bell was covered with the linen napkin and Michael had a firm grip on it.

Taso continued his instructions, saying, "You must now take it, and slowly place the bell over the rail... and let its rim touch the water. Hold on tightly to the bell, and I'll be holding on to you. Do you think you can do it?" he once more asked, and again the answer was "Yes, I can do it!"

Michael turned to the water and edged toward the boat's rail. Taso reached around Michael's waist and tightened his grip. Michael gasped as Taso's strong arms held him tight. "Whenever you're ready, lean over the rail and stretch out and lower the bell to the water."

Michael was ready, as he slowly bent over, bringing the bell closer and closer to the water. The bell was heavy for Michael, and he struggled to keep his balance as he moved it closer to the water. Then suddenly, the boat jolted upward, almost sending the young boy overboard. Michael pulled the bell back into the boat and Taso held even tighter to his waist.

"I'm okay Papa," Michael offered, and once again proceeded to move the bell toward the foaming black water alongside the boat.

Taso was beginning to have second thoughts about putting Michael in such a dangerous situation, but something deep inside kept telling him to proceed on... and that everything would be okay. Taso calmly spoke again to Michael, "Do you still want to do this Michael?" and the child's confident response was, "Yes Papa, I'm going to do it!"

Then once more, Michael approached the rail and started lowering the bell toward the water below the boat. Again, the boat swayed back and forth, pitching in an unexplained fashion. But within Taso's strong grip, Michael was firmly planted against the rail and his balance was secured. As the bell proceeded toward the water, only a hair away from making contact, Taso drew his arms tighter around Michael... and the two were as if one.

Then, Michael closed his eyes, in fear of the unknown that was about to happen. With one last movement, the bell made contact with the water.

An explosion of steam and foam vaporized from the contact of the bell with the water, as if a hot iron skillet was thrust into cold water. Sizzling sounds rushed from the water as boiling thick dark foam rose upward over the bell's rim toward Michael's hands, which were now being covered by freezing black ice. "Hold on Michael," Taso yelled, "It can't hurt you... you have the bell."

Then, as the black foam reached the linen napkin, it instantly retreated back toward the water. Michael continued to lower the bell below the surface, as the sizzling sound continued.

Finally, the bell was submerged to the point where the linen napkin was below the surface. When the napkin was completely covered with the murky water, the water around the bell burst away from its rim, sending high circular waves rushing away from the *Eagles Wing's*, similar to when a pebble is thrown into a still pond, sending circular waves outward from it.

Retreating away from the bell, the waves of thick black water left behind crystal clear blue water in its wake. The huge outward wave continued moving away from the boat, building in height and speed until it had proceeded far beyond sight.

Michael began to open one of his eyes, squinting out to try

to see what had taken place. Then both of his eyes opened, followed by his mother's smile. Michael's arms were straining to hold on to the bell, as fierce hot pain raced up to his shoulders. His nearly frozen hands were barely able to hold on any longer.

"Hold on Michael, we're almost there, the bell is chasing the blackness away" For what seemed to be endless time, Michael held fast to the bell while the black waters retreated in defeat. As long as the bell stayed submerged within the water, the retreat continued. Taso and Michael continued to hold on as the sea around the boat began to smooth out. Finally, all was silent as the confrontation ended.

In exhaustion, Michael's strained arms could barely hold on to the bell as he pleaded with his father... "Papa, I can't hold on any more... what should I do?" Taso knew what had to happen, and gave his son the final instruction... "Let go of the bell my son!"

Michael was confused and surprised at what his father was saying, and replied back, "But Papa, we'll lose it... the water is very deep here and we'll never be able to find it again," as he struggled to hold on with his last bit of strength. Taso again instructed Michael, but this time in a gentle but pleading voice... "Release it Michael, it doesn't belong to us, it belongs to all of mankind, and to the sea where it will protect all of us from any more harm."

Michael couldn't hold on any longer as his small, nearly frozen hands released the bell, but still held on to the linen napkin. For a moment, the bell seemed to hesitate on the surface, as if to allow Michael and Taso to claim a last vision of it. Then, slowly, it drifted downward toward the bottomless crevice... leaving behind warm crystal clear blue water.

Taso fell backward into the boat, drawing Michael into his lap, where they laid there in a silent and motionless embrace.

The morning sun had now peeked over the horizon, sending bright orange and purple bursts of light outward. As Taso and Michael sat sprawled on the deck of the boat, they both knew that something profound and important had happened. Then Taso spoke to Michael, "Are you okay my son?" Michael responded with assurance, "Yes Papa, I'm okay... but I'm not sure what just happened. The bell seemed to chase the black water away... and cleaned up the Cove, even though we lost it... how did it do that?"

Taso just sat there holding on to Michael, and answered, "I don't know myself, but I had a feeling deep inside of me that you, the bell and the Archangel were part of it... and that would be enough to challenge the black water. I guess faith was part of it too... me having faith in what the bell meant, and faith in you and the Archangel. You had faith in me, and we weren't let down. It doesn't matter how everything happened, but more importantly, why it happened the way it did. What matters now is that the water is clean, and I'll bet that the Cove's fishing will get better. As for the bell, it's where it should be, protecting the Cove from whatever may try to hurt it. Man and nature need all the help they can get, and the bell is a special gift to the Cove. Let's leave it where it is, and that'll be our gift to the sea... after all, she's been giving us a lot of gifts, and has made us who we are."

Just then, the sound of another boat could be heard off to the starboard side of the *Eagles Wing's*. Taso and Michael stood up to see what was coming, and lo and behold, there was Tom Moody's boat rushing toward them, sending a spray of water that indicated its urgent speed toward them. Tom slowed his boat as he got closer to the *Eagles Wing's*, and shouted across his bow, "Howdy folks, you guy's okay out here?"

Taso responded by tossing a line to Tom as the boat's lined up side to side. "Yes Tom, were okay... just doing a little more investigation about the black water... but we can't seem to find it anymore." Taso squeezed Michael's shoulder, as if to signal him not to say anything about what had happened before Tom arrived.

Tom looked over his rail, scanning the water around the boat's, and then as far as he could see. To his surprise, the water was calm and crystal clear. "My Lord'y, will ya look at that, I don't think I've ever seen the water that clear before... where did the blackness go?"

Taso and Michael simultaneously shrugged their shoulders, catching themselves as they glanced at one another, and smiled. "Don't have a clue," Taso said, "But I don't care why, it's gone, and that's what's important!"

Tom just stood at the wheel of his boat and continued to stare out over the water. "That's going be good news for the Co-op,

I'll just bet that the fishing is going get better, real quick!" Tom beamed. "Yes Tom, I'm sure it will!" Taso answered as his hands continued to squeeze on Michael's shoulder.

Tom reached for the mooring rope and released it from the cleat, saying, "Well, I'd better get back to the harbor and tell the other fishermen that the water cleared itself and we're ready to fish again... they'll be glad to get out here so they can start paying some bills. I guess you won't have to call those Portland folks anymore," Tom continued as he scratched his head, "I'll never be able to figure out what goes on out here, the sea can sure test one's brain."

Tom's engine came alive as his bow rose from the water and the boat charged toward the harbor. As the boat faded in the distance, Tom's right hand waved back to Taso and Michael who watched the crystal clear blue wake spread out across the Cove.

"Let's go home son, we have a lot to be thankful for," Taso replied as he moved to the pilothouse and fired up the motor, its familiar putt putting sound echoing out from the small boat. A quick glance back to Michael was all that was necessary for him to accept his father's invitation to once again take the wheel, and guide the boat home.

Michael moved into the pilothouse, as his father placed his hands on Michael's shoulders. Michael followed by placing his small chilled hands on the wheel and planting his eyes toward the east. This time, Michael took the throttle and fed the engine fuel as it gained speed and left its own wake behind.

Epilogue

$\mathcal{P}$eace had once again settled on Black Point Cove, and man and nature were in harmony with all of God's creatures. ... but for how long, nobody would know for sure. The lost bell had found a resting place deep within the imeasurable depth of a crevice. Its mysterious hidden presence and power would somehow influence its stewards in ways that they would never know.

These two proud fishermen were heirs to the special gifts that had blessed their lives, as the colorful *Eagles Wing's* lifted upward on the crest of a wave and slipped forward toward home.

Years would pass as Michael and Taso shared the secret of the bell and its mysterious effect on the cove. Eventually Michael became Captain Michael of the *Eagles Wing's* and led the fishing fleet in Black Point Cove. His notoriety as being just like his father and mother were a gift to the community and inspired others to give of their gifts.

Often, when Michael visited his aging father at the house overlooking the cove, he would find Taso staring out of the bay window, overlooking the vast and mysterious ocean. His smile and silence held the secret to life and the depth of love that was knitted within his soul.

Somehow, strange words spoken by an ancient fisherman long ago seemed to whisper in Taso's mind, *"The sounds of man and nature shall never be silenced."* And Michael's bell lying deep in a submerged crevice in Black Point Cove offered comfort and peace to those who received the gifts from the sea.

www.ingramcontent.com/pod-product-compliance
Lightning Source LLC
Chambersburg PA
CBHW052132170626
46812CB00004B/1373